浙江省哲学社会科学重点研究基地
浙江师范大学江南文化研究中心项目

古今越歌英译与评注

An Annotated Anthology of Yue Songs Ancient and Modern

卓振英　编著

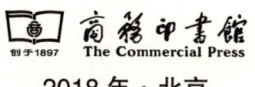

2018 年·北京

图书在版编目（CIP）数据

古今越歌英译与评注 / 卓振英编著．—北京：商务印书馆，2018
ISBN 978-7-100-15787-2

Ⅰ.①古… Ⅱ.①卓… Ⅲ.①诗歌—英语—文学翻译—研究—中国 Ⅳ.① I207.22

中国版本图书馆 CIP 数据核字（2018）第 023612 号

权利保留，侵权必究。

古今越歌英译与评注
卓振英 编著

商务印书馆出版
（北京王府井大街36号 邮政编码100710）
商务印书馆发行
北京市艺辉印刷有限公司印刷
ISBN 978-7-100-15787-2

| 2018年3月第1版 | 开本 880×1230 1/32 |
| 2018年3月北京第1次印刷 | 印张 7 |

定价：32.00 元

目 录
Contents

前　言 ·· 1
Preface

1. 盘古开天辟地歌（无名氏）·· 1
   Eulogy of Pangu for His Creation（Anonymous）
2. 高皇歌（无名氏）·· 4
   Hymn to Emperor Gaoxin（Anonymous）
3. 击壤歌（无名氏）·· 6
   Song of Hit-or-Miss（Anonymous）
4. 弹歌（无名氏）··· 8
   Song of the Catapult（Anonymous）
5. 禹上会稽（姒禹）·· 10
   Chanting atop Mount Kuaiji（Yu the Great）
6. 越人歌（无名氏）·· 13
   The Yue's Song（Anonymous）
7. 渔父歌（无名氏）·· 19
   Song of the Fisherman（Anonymous）
8. 乌鸢歌（越王夫人）··· 22
   Song of the Eagles（Queen of Yue）
9. 吴王女玉歌（姬紫玉）··· 25
   Song of the Princess of Wu（Ji Ziyu）

10. 采葛妇歌（无名氏）··············29
    Gathering Kudzu（Anonymous）
11. 军士离别词（无名氏）············32
    The Soldiers' Pledge on Their Departure（Anonymous）
12. 越人土风歌（无名氏）············34
    The Yues' Song of Their Own Mores（Anonymous）
13. 越谣歌（无名氏）················36
    Ballad of the Yues（Anonymous）
14. 曹娥姞（无名氏）················38
    What a Good Lass（Anonymous）
15. 会稽童谣（无名氏）··············40
    A Children's Rhyme of Kuaiji（Anonymous）
16. 徐圣通歌（无名氏）··············42
    Ode to Xu Shengtong（Anonymous）
17. 太湖神之歌（无名氏）············44
    Song of the God of the Taihu Lake（Anonymous）
18. 咏鹅（骆宾王）··················46
    Song to the Goose（Luo Binwang）
19. 杂歌（无名氏）··················48
    One of the Mescellaneous Songs（Anonymous）
20. 相思曲（刘三姐）················50
    A Song of the Pursuit of Love（Liu Sanjie）
21. 骂财主（刘三姐）················53
    Denouncing the Cruel Landlord（Liu Sanjie）
22. 财主心肠比蛇毒（刘三姐）········55
    The Rich Are Even More Poisonous than the Snake（Liu Sanjie）
23. 采茶歌（刘三姐）················57
    Tea-Picking Song（Liu Sanjie）

24. 山中只见藤缠树（刘三姐）·················61
　　The Tree in th' Mount a Vine's Seen to Enlace（Liu Sanjie）

25. 竹子当收你不收（刘三姐）·················62
　　If Grown Bamboos You Fail in Time to Reap（Liu Sanjie）

26. 渔家傲（汪东）·················63
　　Pride of the Fisherman（Wang Dong）

27. 吴越王还乡歌（钱镠）·················65
　　Song of a Prince's Return（Qian Liu）

28. 婺州山中人歌（无名氏）·················68
　　Song of the Man in the Mounts（Anonymous）

29. 月子弯弯（无名氏）·················70
　　The Crescent Moon（Anonymous）

30. 嫁鸡随鸡（无名氏）·················72
　　Inflicted Marriages（Anonymous）

31. 采桑曲（郑震）·················74
　　Picking Mulberry Leaves（Zheng Zhen）

32. 树旗谣（无名氏）·················76
　　Song of Revolt（Anonymous）

33. 越歌（宋濂）·················78
　　A Yue Song（Song Lian）

34. 汤绍恩歌（无名氏）·················80
　　Song to Tang Shao'en（Anonymous）

35. 赞花瓦氏征倭（无名氏）·················82
　　Song in Praise of Madame Wa（Anonymous）

36. 送别歌（无名氏）·················84
　　Antiphonal about Madame Wa（Anonymous）

37. 重逢（节选）（无名氏）·················86
　　Reunion (excerpt)（Anonymous）

38. 马桑树儿搭灯台（无名氏）··················· 88
    Th' Masang Embraces th' Lampstand with Delight（Anonymous）

39. 官贼歌（叶子奇）··················· 91
    The Robber and the Official（Ye Ziqi）

40. 喜鹊歌（胡温）··················· 93
    Song of the Magpie（Hu Wen）

41. 职方贱如狗（无名氏）··················· 95
    As Dogs Army Inspectors Are as Cheap（Anonymous）

42. 怨天歌（无名氏）··················· 97
    Grievance Against Heaven（Anonymous）

43. 天上星多月不明（无名氏）··················· 99
    Too Many Stars in the Sky Will Tarnish the Moon（Anonymous）

44. 长毛到西兴（无名氏）··················· 101
    The Long-hair'd Having Come to Xixing（Anonymous）

45. 诸暨何文庆（无名氏）··················· 104
    Eulogy of He Wenqing（Anonymous）

46. 宝刀歌（无名氏）··················· 106
    Song of the Sword（Anonymous）

47. 嵊县有个牛大王（无名氏）··················· 108
    Our Hero from th' Sheng County（Anonymous）

48. 辛亥革命山歌（无名氏）··················· 110
    A Folk Song of the Xinhai Revolution（Anonymous）

49. 送郎当红军（无名氏）··················· 113
    I Send You, Darling, to the Red Army（Anonymous）

50. 新四军军歌（陈毅、叶挺等）··················· 115
    Anthem of the New Fourth Army（Chen Yi, Ye Ting et al.）

51. 松竹茶山升红旗（无名氏）··················· 120
    Red Flags Are Waving in the Songzhu Tea Mounts（Anonymous）

52. 保卫新昌（无名氏）……123
    In Defence of Xinchang（Anonymous）

53. 龙山中学校歌（梁荫源）……125
    Anthem of Longshan Middle School（Liang Yinyuan）

54. 四明山（无名氏）……128
    Song of the Siming Mounts（Anonymous）

55. 共产党像亲娘（无名氏）……131
    The Party Has Given Us Lots of Motherly Care（Anonymous）

56. 三五支队威名扬（无名氏）……133
    The Third and Fifth Detachments Are Known Far and Wide（Anonymous）

57. 地下无笑声（无名氏）……135
    On the Earth No Laughter Can Be Heard（Anonymous）

58. 浏阳河（湖南省文工团歌舞队）……137
    Song of the Liuyang Rill（HAT Song and Dance Team）

59. 洪湖水，浪打浪（梅少山、张敬安等）……141
    The Surging Waves Foam and Break（Mei Shaoshan, Zhang Jing'an et al.）

60. 毛主席，最公平（无名氏）……144
    Chairman Mao Is Really Nice and Fair（Anonymous）

61. 永远涨来永远明（无名氏）……146
    Unfathomable Are th' Waters in th' Seas（Anonymous）

62. 十穷歌（无名氏）……148
    Ten Causes of Poverty（Anonymous）

63. 转娘家（无名氏）……151
    Visiting with My Parents（Anonymous）

64. 思娘猛（无名氏）……153
    For Mom My Yearning's Deep（Anonymous）

65. 情姐下河洗衣裳（无名氏）……………………………155
   My Sweet Is Washing on the Rill（Anonymous）

66. 月亮婆婆（无名氏）………………………………………157
   Granny Moon（Anonymous）

67. 呵痒（无名氏）……………………………………………158
   A Rhyme of Tickling（Anonymous）

68. 拍拍心（无名氏）…………………………………………160
   A Ditty of Patting（Anonymous）

69. 摇，摇，摇（无名氏）……………………………………162
   I Row, Row and Row（Anonymous）

70. 爱拼才会赢（陈百潭）……………………………………164
   He Wins Who Relies on Himself and Takes Pains（Chen Baitan）

附录……………………………………………………………167
   Appendixes

主要参考文献…………………………………………………183
   References

前　言

　　从远古时代开始，南方诸族便在秦岭及淮河以南繁衍生息。《汉书·地理志》颜师古（581—645）注引臣瓒曰："自交趾至会稽七八千里，百越杂处，各有种姓"。对于这些种姓，历史上有多种称谓。夏代（约前21—前16世纪）称之为"越"，商代（前1600—前1046）称之为"蛮越"或"南越"，周代（前1046—前256）称之为"荆越""扬越"，战国时期（前475—前221）则称之为"百越"（或写为"百粤"，"越""粤"互通）。"百越"一词沿用至今，它一般用以指称这些种姓，包括东越、瓯人、于越、扬越、姑妹、海阳、损子、九菌、越常、骆越、瓯越、瓯皑、且瓯、西瓯、供人、目深、摧夫、禽人、苍吾、越区、桂国、产里、海癸、稽余、北带、仆句和区吴，等等；有时也可用以指称他们所生活的地域，其范围"当在今日之浙江绍兴至越南北部"（冯明洋，2006：63），即当今之江苏、浙江、湖北、湖南、安徽、江西、福建、广东、广西、海南及越南北部。

　　百越人"具有共同的体质特征（南亚蒙古人种体质）和共同的文化特征（几何印纹陶文化）"（冯明洋，2006：64）。他们断发文身，山居野处；以舟为车，以楫为马；往若飘风，去则难从；契臂为盟，多食海产；惯于水战，善铸铜器（如青铜剑、铜铎）。楚越故地是春秋战国时代青铜宝剑的故乡。楚王派人寻访铸剑名师，终于找到了欧冶子（公元前514年前后）。欧冶子在当今的浙江龙泉凿开茨山，将溪泉引到铸剑炉旁的七星池中，用以淬火。因炼成的宝剑仿若卧龙，故取名"七星龙渊剑"。福建福州古代称为冶城，相传城中的冶山也是欧冶子铸剑的地方。据《越绝书·越绝外传记宝剑》所载，欧冶子耗时三年，在湛卢山（今福建松溪县）炼出天下第一名剑"湛卢"。浙江莫干山系得名于名剑干将、莫邪。1965年在湖北出土一把越王勾践的宝剑，1973年在湖北江陵又出土一把越王州句剑。

百越人所使用的古越语与北方的古汉语相差极大，彼此不能通话。百越语为黏着型，不同于汉语的单音成义。根据语言学者的研究，吴语、闽语和粤语与古越语有相当密切的关系。

清代学者屈大均（1630—1696）在他的《广东新语》中指出，"粤俗好歌，凡有吉庆，必唱歌以为欢乐"。书中提到，唐中宗年间，"新兴女子有刘三妹者，相传为始造（山歌）之人……淹通经史，善为歌"。

越人同中原的交流"早在商周时期已有记载"（冯明洋，2006：89），他们以象牙、玳瑁、翠毛、犀角、玉桂和香木等交换自己所需的北方产品。《庄子》里有一则笑话，说有个北人把帽子运到越地去贩卖，其结果是无功而返，因为断发文身的越人没有戴帽子的习惯。于此可见，古越族和北方确实很早就有贸易等文化联系。百越曾从属于楚，"其见证就是在番禺（今广州）建立的'楚庭'。楚庭相传为楚威王时期（前339—前329）的"楚相高固所建"，是楚国行使、宣示其管辖权的行政机关。（冯明洋，2006：90）

百越有着悠久的文明史。浙江五万年前即有原始人"建德人"的活动。余姚河姆渡出土的七千年前新石器时期文物（稻谷、骨哨、骨耜等）证明，百越是稻作文化起源地之一，百越民族是世界上最早饲养家猪的古老民族之一。广西百色盆地出土过手斧等石制品。2000年，美国加利福尼亚伯克利地质年代中心的一位地质年代学家在该地采集到与这些石制品共存的陨石，并用"钾-氩法"进行测定，得出的结论是，那些石器的制造年代大约在80.3万年前。美国加利福尼亚大学的一位古人类学家说，年代的确定解决了长期困扰着国际考古界的重大难题，这使得考古界不得不对亚洲人类文明起源进行重新评估。福建一带在远古时代就生活着属于海洋蒙古利亚人种的原始人类，到了3000年前，他们已经创造出独具一格的原始文化。1958年，在广东韶关市曲江区马坝镇西南两千米处的狮子岩发现"马坝人"的头盖骨。"马坝人"是12.9万年前旧石器时代的古人类，介于中国猿人和现代人之间。据推测，其脑容量比北京人大。1972年，在"马坝人"出土地点的两山之间又发现了距今约四五千年前新石器时期的文化遗址，考古界称与之相关的文化为"石峡文化"。广东潮安陈桥曾经发现距今5000年至6000年的贝丘（shell mound）文化遗存，与福州平潭所发现的遗存相同。广东普宁后山也曾经发现距今3500年至4000年的文化遗存。考古学家研究发现，"在今闽南漳州、漳浦、东山至粤东南澳一线，距今9000年至13000年之间，已存在一条文化流动线"（冯明洋，2006：196）。湖南多处发现史前遗址，如2006年发掘的辰溪溪口史前贝丘遗址。其他南方省份的类似发现不胜枚举。

　　斗换星移，随着历史变迁，百越先民所创造的百越文化，与中原文化、荆楚文化、北方文化、东夷文化一道，汇聚成了博大精深、灿烂辉煌的中华文化。

　　有史以来，祖国的南方人杰地灵，圣哲英才辈出，文化成就辉煌。然而，以亲缘关系为因子之一的周朝王家正统思想以及嗣后的封建王朝的傲慢与偏见,或多或少地影响着对于南方的历史评价。利用文献、语言进行一番考古,我们就不难发现这一点。这里可以举两个简单的例子加以说明。楚蛮、荆蛮、南夷、南蛮、南蛮𫛡舌等词语在其最初使用时显然是带有歧视色彩的;尽管楚国地域广大、文化辉煌、国力强盛,但在正史中,其国君依旧被呼为"楚子",楚史也得不到应有的篇幅;《楚辞》是世界文化瑰宝,朱熹说它"过于中庸"(即背离中庸之道)、"不知学于北方,以求周公仲尼之道,而独驰骋于变风变雅之末流"(《楚辞集注·序》),批评者的哲学道德标准和立场也毫不含糊。楚人的历史同样可以说明这一点。正是由于如此,对楚史做一粗略回顾就绝非多余。

在商朝的挤压驱逐之下,帝高阳之苗裔、祝融后裔八姓之一的芈姓部族不得不从发源地有熊之墟(约在今之河南新郑)迁徙至豫西南、陕东南和丹淅流域,几经辗转,才落脚于荆山一带。因部族助周灭商,首领鬻熊(又称鬻熊子)当了周文王的火师。他是已知最早的道家人物之一,著有《鬻子》[①]。他认为,"发教施令,为天下福者谓之道";"欲刚必以柔守之,欲强必以弱保之。积于柔必刚,积于弱必强。观其所积,以知祸福之乡";"物损于彼者盈于此,成于此者亏于彼。损盈成亏,随生随死"。这种以民为本、辩证变易的道学思想为后来的老子(李聃,楚人)、孔子(前551—前479)、庄子(庄周,楚国王族后裔,约前369—前286)、屈原[②](楚国王族后裔,约前340—前278)等贤哲所继承,分别发展成

---

① 刘勰《文心雕龙·诸子》曰:"至鬻熊知道,文王咨询,余文遗事,录为《鬻子》。"有唐代逢行珪注的明正统道藏本《鬻子》传世。
② 屈原乃世界文化名人,古来赞颂之诗文汗牛充栋。今人又有《端午怀屈子》一诗云:形御清波去,神从圣哲游。至今思正气,赫赫照千秋!

为道家以及儒家的核心思想"仁"的学说，也对楚国产生过影响。在某种意义上可以说，楚国是道家的发源地。

在周王朝裂土分封的诸多决定因素中，亲缘关系重于历史功绩。周成王念及鬻熊的贡献，封其曾孙熊绎（前1042—前1006）为子爵，封地50里（相当于20平方公里）。熊绎作为楚国封君，跋山涉水前往参加分封后举行的称为"岐阳之搜"的会盟，结果不但无资格入席，而且还被使唤去干些杂差。其后人对此类待遇颇有微词："昔我先王熊绎，与吕级、王孙牟、燮父、禽父，并事康王，四国皆有分，我独无有"；"昔我先王熊绎，辟在荆山，筚路蓝缕，以处草莽。跋涉山林，以事天子。唯是桃弧、棘矢，以共御王事。齐，王舅也。晋及鲁、卫，王母弟也。楚是以无分，而彼皆有。"（《左传·昭公十二年》）由于楚的身份与地位长期得不到周王朝的承认，楚武王索性封子为王。

楚人爵位虽低（子爵），却是列国中最有作为的。他们自强不息，艰苦创业，努力进取，从开始的"筚路蓝缕，以启山林"，发展到庄王（？—前591）时期的一鸣惊人、位居霸主，这与楚国的治国方略不无关系。楚武王（？—前690）"大启群蛮"，开发江汉，与其后继者先后兼并了邓国、绞国、权国、罗国、申国、随国、息国、贰国、谷国、弦国、黄国、英国、蒋国、道国、柏国、房国、轸国、夔国等诸侯国，其间自然难免征战，但若没有适合时宜的文化战略、包容开放的思想和"为天下福"的政治举措，其领土必将得而复失。楚人一方面通过变革创新，改造了他们带来的先进的中原文化，使之本土化以适应新的土壤，另一方面对土著文化采取包容的态度，尊重具有不同信仰、习俗和传统的族群，并将合乎时宜的苗蛮文化因子兼收并蓄，形成了朝气蓬勃、辉煌璀璨的荆楚文化。从习俗看，崇火尚赤是楚人自身的文化因子，与其祖先祝融有关；喜巫近鬼则是天人合一的信念与百越、荆蛮的巫文化结合之后形成的，有利于处在险恶环境中的人类的生存、发展；凤凰的美好形象是在"善"的理念和文化自觉意识指导下文化创新的产物，尊凤有利于凝聚较为普遍地信奉鸟图腾的南方部族，推行启蒙教化，培养文化自尊与认同①。楚国在其全盛时期地域广大（所辖地域大致覆盖当今的湖北、湖南全部，以及重庆、贵州、河南、安徽、江苏、江西、浙江、广东等省的全部或部分），文化发达，物产丰富，人才济济，国力强盛。开放、包容、创新所产生的文化活力促进了楚国的政治、社会和经济发展。例如，楚国兼并扬越之后，用越人之所长，令其从事冶炼、铸造工作，大大提高了楚国青铜业的生产力，使楚国得以在青铜器制造方面超越其他诸侯国。虽然周昭王（？—前1002）曾两次兴师讨伐荆楚，齐国也以"楚贡包茅不入，王祭不备"为由对楚出兵，但都未能遏制楚的发展。作为泱泱大国，楚国的哲学在深度与思辨性方面都可与几乎同时期的古希腊（前800—前146）媲美，天文、历法、文学、音乐、雕刻、绘画等都达到很高的水平，世界上第一段长城、第一支毛笔、第一个县级行政设置都出自楚，所有这一切都毫不足怪。在探讨楚国的发展壮大时，黄瑞云先生在《楚国论》中、张正明先生

---

① 鸟形图像普遍存在于长江流域的原始遗存中，例如，河姆渡遗址就发现了双鸟朝阳象牙雕刻、鸟形象牙雕刻、圆雕木鸟以及刻有双头连体鸟纹图像的骨匕。在中国南方的古代民族中，越人的图腾标志主要是鸟。居住在山东、江苏一带的东方各种夷人最初也是以崇拜鸟为主，如少昊部落的凤鸟氏、玄鸟氏、青鸟氏、丹鸟氏等。民族志的材料说明，大多数近现代少数民族都还或多或少地残留有鸟图腾崇拜的文化痕迹。怒族、苗族、满族、朝鲜族等都有鸟图腾，有的还流传着关于鸟是自己祖先的神话。此外，黎族、珞巴族、赫哲族也都有鸟图腾，彝族有在门上挂一只鹰以避邪的习俗。

在《楚文化史》中都谈及其宽容、开放与仁慈。有学者指出，楚在兼并小国后往往保存其国君宗庙，安抚其人民，也从没有像秦那样对待战俘。据刘向（约前77—前6）《说苑》的记载，驾舟的越人用越语所唱的《越人歌》被翻译为楚语后，位居令尹、爵为执圭的鄂君（子皙）"乃揄修袂，行而拥之，举绣被而覆之"，于此可见楚国王族对于越族亲善友好的一面。作为王族后裔的屈原尊重越文化，吸取越歌的养分，使之成为《楚辞》的艺术源头之一。

由是观之，周王朝对楚的傲慢与偏见不容否认；楚国之所以强盛，之所以能够在文化大融合中扮演重要角色，是其哲学、文化、政治、地理等诸多因素使然，其中民族性格上的刚性永远具有借鉴意义。若不是前期采取刚柔相济的战略取向，对周王朝的歧视、挤压只是一味屈从忍让，则楚将不楚。

楚越历来交好。文化交流方面，楚康王时就有越女赴楚演唱越歌（朱秋枫，2004：22）；政治关系方面，两国存在由联姻所强化的联盟；人才交流方面，楚人在越为官的有计倪、文种、范蠡、陈音，越人在楚为官的有庄舃，等等。所有这些都为后来的文化融合铺平了道路。

公元前306年，楚国兼并越国，楚越进一步融合。这不仅大大促进了江南社会、经济和文化的发展，对于多民族国家的形成和壮大也有着十分重大的意义。若干年后，南方美丽温柔的凤凰，与北方吉祥刚强的神龙风云际会，南北一统，龙凤呈祥，终于形成了天人合一、以人为本、宽厚包容、刚柔相济、博大精深、异彩纷呈的中国文化，营造了五十六个兄弟民族山青水秀、天宽地阔、温馨融和的共同家园。一个热爱和平的大国的形成必然将成为世界和平的福音。

这里要顺带一提的是，几千年形成的农耕文化带有讲和不讲争、知守不知攻、阴柔有余而阳刚不足等文化缺陷，这些缺陷给自身惹来不少外患,极其不利于民族的生存发展。作为中国人,在弱肉强食、新法西斯主义和霸权主义越来越猖獗的世界环境中,若不进行一番深刻的文化反省,并适当借鉴、吸收海洋文化、狩猎文化、游牧文化传统中的刚性因子,恐怕是十分危险的。

虽然古越人已经"一去不复返",越文化却得到了传承和发展。研究者发现,越地在古今风俗方面有很多相通之处。从周处(236—297)《风土记》中的越俗看,"弹圆盘而舞和祭祀用猪牛与现今瑶族、畲族的风俗习惯极为相似,可见记述这些南方风俗时,记录者尚将瑶族、畲族等南方少数民族,一律谓之'越人'、'越俗'"(朱秋枫,2004:50)。现今有关区域之间在歌乐等方面也有同一性,例如,"现在的象州壮族民歌"中平调"同浙江临安民歌《百客因》,不仅曲调相似,而且上下句的落音行腔几乎相同";"罗城仫佬族民歌'土拐歌'同浙江定海、仙居民歌的曲调也有许多相似之处";广西民歌"玉林大山歌"与江苏吴县民歌"吴县调"如出一辙(冯明洋,2006:26);《中国民间歌曲集成》浙江卷与广东卷中的两种《高皇歌》"高度同一",只是广东的"潮州调"更像《高皇歌》的原生形态(冯明洋,2006:332—333)。在谈及"古瓯歌与浙闽交接地区歌谣的地方特色"时,朱秋枫总结出以下几点:使用衬词、衬句;句式、歌体自由而又有一定规制;形式丰富多彩;风格古朴自在。(朱秋枫,2004:242—344)

实际上,江南各地歌谣,包括壮族民歌,几乎都具有这些特点。《浏阳河》一歌是采用湖南花鼓调谱的曲,它与浙江的《四明山》在题材方面一则以水,一则以山,有问有答,二者形式颇多共性。我们可以再比较一下浙江的《转娘家》与广西同一题材的瑶歌《思娘猛》:

因转娘家脚头轻,　　　　　思娘猛,
微微细雨也是晴;　　　　　行路也思睡也思,
远远路外也是近,　　　　　行路思娘留半路,
爬山过岭也是平。　　　　　睡也思娘留半床。

显而易见,二者在句法、结构、表现手法上确有异曲同工之妙。

可见百越之地的历代歌谣并非无源之水、无本之木,古今越歌的传承关系密切。正如冯明洋所指出的,岭南歌乐"不管汇入多少新元素、新声源,其韵致中总是渗透着来自本根源头的越土越水之乡情乡音。这种既有整体感、连续感,又有相对独立性、自主性及稳定性的乡情乡音,……的越风越韵总是主流。"(冯明洋,2006:20)"尽管外形多变,但其内核……相当稳定。特别是特性音调,作为种族记忆符号,将以集体无意识的形式恒久传承。"(冯明洋,2006:23)明代学者宋濂(1310—1381)创作了《越歌》;清人有关著作收录了历代(包括清代)越歌,例如,"粤风""瑶歌""俍歌""獞歌""杂歌"等五卷歌谣被吴淇(1615—1675)、赵龙文等收编于《粤风续九》;娄子匡(1914—2005)、裘士雄(1943—)分别于1931年和2001年出版的同名歌谣集《越歌百曲》,也都包含了春秋战国之后流传于百越之地的歌谣。现今浙江、广东、广西、湖南等地的越歌是当中较有特色的歌乐形式,有着自己的独特魅力。

越歌具有如下文化品格:其一,主体性品格,即以自然为基础的人生本位取向;其二,民族性品格,即以家庭为基础的群体本位取向;其三,规范性品格,即以伦理为基础的礼仪本位取向;其四,内向性品格,即以个性为基础的整合本位取向。(冯明洋,2006:51—55)

朱秋枫指出，"对越歌影响最为深远的是楚文化"，"古越歌是越楚文化长期交融的一种产物。"（朱秋枫，2004：12—13）为了揭示越歌与楚歌的内在联系，朱秋枫从二者抽样并进行了比较：

秋兰兮青青，　　　　　　今夕何夕兮，
绿叶兮紫茎。　　　　　　搴舟中流；
满堂兮美人，　　　　　　今日何日兮，
忽独与余兮目成！　　　　得与王子同舟！
　　（《少司命》）　　　　　　（《越人歌》）

沅有芷兮澧有兰，　　　　山有木兮木有枝，
思公子兮未敢言！　　　　心悦君兮君不知！
　　（《湘夫人》）　　　　　　（《越人歌》）

他归纳道，二者"不仅句式韵味极其相似，而且在景物与感情的描述上，也有某些相通之处"。他还以《国殇》与《军士离别词》为例，指出二者"在表现风格上也是相近的"（朱秋枫，2004：13）。

有关越歌的记载散见于各种书籍中，诸如汉代刘向所著的《说苑》、赵晔所著的《吴越春秋》，晋代周处的《风土记》、干宝（？—336）的《搜神记》、郭璞（276—324）的《临安地志》、虞预（约285—340）的《会稽典录》、南朝沈约（441—513）的《宋书》、萧子显（487—537）的《南齐书》，唐代房玄龄（579—648）的《晋书》、释道宣（596—667）的《续高僧传》，等等。清代一些有眼光的学者开始瞩目于越歌的整理和研究。在这方面，吴淇与赵龙文等编著的《粤风续九》、李调元（1734—1803）编著的《粤风》（广西各族民间

情歌集）似为滥觞之作。20世纪20年代至80年代，民俗学界、歌谣学界、音乐学界对越地民歌进行了记录、整理和研究，成就斐然。在当代较有影响的著作中，朱秋枫的《浙江歌谣源流史》分门别类，断代明确，资料丰富，分析中肯，来龙去脉，一清二楚；冯明洋的《越歌——岭南本土歌乐文化论》则从史学、考古学、音乐学、文化人类学等多学科视角论证了古今越歌的传承关系，并深入探讨了岭南越歌的渊源、特色、流布和发展，可谓史论合璧。

作为文化的有声艺术载体，越歌以最活跃的形式，广泛、恒久地存活在民间，折射出古代江南的社会、历史、文学、哲学、语言、民俗、信仰乃至天文、地理等风貌，被誉为"社会生活的百科全书""民族精神的档案"①。

文化是民族的灵魂，典籍是文化的有形载体。一个民族的典籍外译，与该民族的生存发展、文化身份、文化活力、文化传承、文化安全、经典新生、抵御霸权等息息相关，意义重大。（卓振英，2011：6—8）珍视越歌这一人类非物质文化遗产，进一步加以发掘、研究，并通过英译而赋予它新的生命形态和生存空间，这无疑是很有意义的。基于这种认识，本研究选取先秦至当代部分越歌，予以翻译、评注，以图勾画出越歌之概貌，映射出越文化之辉煌。评注提供背景知识，说明出处并分析越歌的表现手法。

一个好的典籍译者应该具有"上善若水"、"水利万物而不争"（老子《道德经》）的品格，为和平治学，为天下立言。唯有如此，方能在典籍翻译中如切如磋、精益求精、严谨治学，而绝不会急功近利、粗制滥造、欺世盗名、以量取

---

① 参看乔建中为冯明洋《越歌：岭南本土歌乐文化论》一书所作的序言（第2页）。

胜乃至于从事理论造假、以权术玩弄学术，因为那样将前亵渎了古人、后有负于来者。"夫孰非义而可用兮，孰非善而可服？"（屈原《离骚》）

一个好的典籍译者还应力求具有远见卓识，能够提出引领学术发展的思路与见解，做一个胸怀博大的思想者。这样，只要关于典籍英译的问题与对策、关于建立全国典籍英译研究会等策略与思想能够得以推行，就会怀着"待到山花烂漫时，她在丛中笑"（毛泽东《卜算子·咏梅》）的心胸，辱而不怒，扼而不衰，坦然地对待压制和挫折。"苟余情其信姱以练要兮，长顑颔亦何伤？"（屈原《离骚》）

一个好的典籍译者还应该具有基本的东西方文化知识和语言基础，否则就可能会把《上邪》中的"君"理解为"heaven above"，把"长命无绝衰"翻译为"Let it endure despite the fates above"，或在"典籍"前添上"文化"这一蛇足。

基于以上认识，本书在翻译、评注方面力求严谨。例如，书中提及的历史人物上百人，典籍也不下几十部；为了贴切妥当地翻译出书名、尽可能精确地提供作者的生卒时间，编著者都是在经过一番认真查考之后方才动笔的。

思想与学术上应做到"百花齐放，百家争鸣"。就某一典籍而言，不同的英译共存互补，可构成互文网络，有助于读者从不同的视角观照、理解元典。再者，他山之石，可以攻玉，作为典籍译者，应该虚心学习他人的长处。基于这些考虑，在可能、必要的情况下，本书将为读者提供不同的译作。

我在本书中将不揣冒昧，本着社会责任意识和与读者交流的目的，谈谈自己在文化方面的一些思考。为了降低注释的厚重感，这些思考连同对文本及歌词的辨析、考证（例如《越人歌》中有关歌者的性别以及"绣被"的含义的探讨）置于附录中。

越歌翻译是在诗学范式理论指导下进行的，该理论的代表作是《汉诗英译论纲》（详见"主要参考资料"）。

本书的所谓"越歌"是广义的，指的是产生、流传于百越之地的历代民歌。把该区域在近当代所产生的民歌归类于越歌的范畴是顺理成章的，其依据就是上文所提及的传承关系以及歌谣学界的共识。所选的越地各族（包括汉族、壮族、仡佬族、畲族、瑶族等）歌谣在形式上多种多样，有独唱、对唱、并唱、重唱、合唱，有三行体、四行体、五行体、六行体等；在内容上丰富多彩，有创世歌、功德歌、刺邪歌、劝世歌、爱恋歌、交友歌、嬉戏歌、民俗歌、劳作歌等。歌谣尽量按其产生的年代顺序编排，不过，由于不少越歌的传承方式是口传心授，至少在目前是无法确切断定其产生年代的，因而歌谣所涉及的事件便成为确定编排次序的另一主要因素。将《盘古开天辟地歌》作为首篇就是考虑到这一因素。

主客观因素决定了本选集的局限性。主观方面，编著者对于越歌的知识积累贫薄，鞭长莫及之处定然不少。客观方面，现存研究多数是对某个民族或某一区域越歌的记录、整理和描述，其范畴尚未涵盖整个百越地区，这就在选材上造成了极大的困难；再者，在越歌英译方面，零散的越歌英译尚属罕见，结集出版并加以评注更无先例，这就使得选材、英译及评注无所参照。作为越歌外译的初步尝试，本集所采撷的只是越歌百花园中一小束奇葩，还缺乏广泛性、代表性和典型性。虽然英译力求遵循"以诗译诗"的原则，最大限度地再现原作音韵美、形式美、风格美、情感美、思想美和意境美，评注也力求中肯贴切，但由于译者功力有限，料难尽如人意。期望读者、方家不吝指教。

浙江省哲学社会科学重点研究基地"江南文化研究中心"为本研究立项并提供了出版资助；浙江师大外语学院党政

领导、陈玉兰教授、陈昌义教授、陈其强教授、周林东教授以及典籍英译研究所的同事都曾给我以宝贵的鼓励与支持；徐微洁博士不计功利，高效优质地为本书做了部分翻译工作；商务印书馆许晓娟编辑的认真严谨令我受益匪浅；学术界的朋友、各类参考资料作者及网站为本研究提供了宝贵的资料和信息。在此谨向以上单位和个人致以诚挚的谢意！

卓振英

2015年4月30日完成初稿

2015年11月18日改定于

浙江师范大学典籍英译研究所

Preface

Thousands of years ago, there lived in the vast areas south to the Qinling Mountains and the Huai River a multitude of tribes, who were termed the "Yues" in the Xia Dynasty (appr. 2100−1600 BC), the "Uncivilized Yues" or "Southern Yues" in the Shang Dynasty (1600−1046 BC), the "Jin Yues" or the "Yang Yues" in the Zhou Dynasty (1046−256 BC), and the "Multitude of Yues" during the Warring States Period (475−221 BC). The expression "The Multitude of Yues", which is still in use today, may refer to those ancient tribesmen, or to the areas they lived in, which should have included the present-day Jiangsu, Zhejiang, Hubei, Hunan, Anhui, Jiangxi, Fujian, Guangdong, Guangxi and Hainan, a coverage running from Kuaiji of today's Zhejiang to the north of the present Vietnam." (Feng Mingyang, 2006: 63) Just as Chenzan (of the Jin Dynasty) says, "In the areas totaling around seven to eight thousand square *li*, running from Jiaozhi to Kuaiji, there lived a multitude of races called the Yues," which is quoted by Yan Shigu (581−645) in a note to The Geographical Sketches of *The Book of the Han Dynasty*. The races were known as the Eastern Yue, the Ouren, the Yuyue, the Yangyue, the Gumei, the Haiyang, the Sunzi, the Jiujun, the Yuechang, the Luoyue, the Ouyue, the Ou'ai, the Qie'ou, the

Weastern Ou, the Gongren, the Mushen, the Cuifu, the Qinren, the Cangwu, the Yue'ou, the Guiguo, the Chanli, the Haigui, the Jiyu, the Beidai, the Puju, the Ouwu, etc. in accordance with historical records.

The Yues, "sharing the physical distinctions of the Southern Mongolian Race, had the same cultural features." (Feng Mingyang, 2006: 64) They tended to be tattooed and have their hair cut; they mostly dwelled in rugged mountainous regions, moved about by boats, loved sea food, and were swift in action and adept in warfares on water; and they were good at manufacturing bronze ware, such as bronze swords and bronze bells. Facts and archaeological findings show that the regions of Wu and Yue had been the home of bronze swords during the Spring and Autumn Period (770-476 BC), which speaks for the fact that Mount Mogan has derived its name from the famous swords Ganjiang and Moye; when it annexed the Yangyue, the State of Chu employed the Yues in bronze sword manufacturing; and unearthed respectively in 1965 and 1973 were Goujian's Zhouju's sabers. Ou Yezi, a renowned expert of Chu in sword manufacturing, had his sword manufacturing centers in Longquan of Zhejiang and Fuzhou of Fujian.

The adhesive-type language of the ancient Yues is quite different from the ancient Chinese spoken by the northerners. The researches of linguists have verified that today's dialects of Wu (吴, approximately the present Jiangsu), Min (闽, i.e. the present Fujian) and Yue (粤, i.e. the present Guangdong) have a close relation with the language of the ancient Yues.

There is a joke in *Zhuangzi*[①] telling that a northerner transported some hats to the region of Yue for sale, and that consequently his goods didn't sell, for the Yues never wore hats. From that we can see the Yues had had cultural ties with the north long long before. Trade contacts and cultural intercourses began "as early as the Shang Dynasty". (Feng Mingyang, 2006: 89) The Yues had come under the jurisdiction of Chu, and the administration center the Court of Chu (built approximately in the fourth century BC by Chu's prime minister Gao Gu), situated in what is today's Guangzhou, may serve as a piece of evidence.

The Multitude of Yues boasts of a long history. Around fifty thousand years before, the primitive "Jiande Men" had lived in the present Zhejiang. The neolithic relics unearthed at Hemudu, such as unhusked rice, bone spades and bone flutes, have manifested that the Multitude of Yues is one of the first races in raising pigs, and the areas they lived in is one of the sources of rice culture. In 2000, an American scholar found out through testing that such relics as hand axes discovered in Bose of Guangxi are at least of 803,000 years old in geological time, which, just as an American paleoanthropologist points out, has prompted the archaeological circle to re-assess the beginning of Asian civilization. In 1958, the fossil of a skull of the Maba Hominid, a protolithic human race living 129,000 years ago, was excavated in Shaoguan of Guangdong. In 1972, some 5000-year-old

---

[①] *Zhuangzi*, written by Zhuang Zhou (庄周 , 369–286 BC), is a classic in the philosophy of Daoism.

neolithic relics were unearthed. Such archaeological findings as shell mounds, at Puning and Chao'an of Guangdong, as well as those at Pingtan of Fujian, have pointed to the fact that "a belt of cultural flow, extending from the present-day Southern Fujian (including Zhangzhou, Zhangpu and Dongshan) to Nan'ao of Guangdong, had existed 9,000 to 13,000 years before." (Feng Mingyang, 2006: 196) Pre-historical shell mounds and other relics, such as the one excavated in Chenxi, Hunan, have been unearthed in the other southern provinces.

Stars are revolving, and constellations are in constant changes. In the course of cultural exchanges and historical developments, the Yue culture has converged with the Central Plain culture (中原文化), the Jing-Chu culture (荆楚文化), the Dongyi culture (东夷文化) and the Northern culture (北方文化), and thus become a component part of the profound and magnificent Chinese culture.

The heroic people of the south, from the great sages and philosophers to the rank and file, have lent incomparable charm and glory to their homeland. Notwithstanding that, the evaluation of the south has more or less been affected by the orthodox ideas, which bear the gene of affiliation, as well as by the pride and prejudice of the northern dynasties. A simple archaeological survey through language and literature would shed light on the point. Such expressions as "the savage south" and "the savage Chu" evidently had a connotation of discrimination when they were first put to use; The Verse of Chu, an immortal classic, was rebuked for its "transgression of the Principle of the Mean" and "failure in abiding by the doctrines advocated by the Duke of

Zhou and Confucius." The history of Chu may also verify the case. As regards that point, to catch a glimpse of Chu's growth is not bringing owls to Athens.

Driven by the Shang Dynasty, the tribesmen with the family name of Mi, as descendants of Emperor Gaoyang (高阳) and one of the eight branches of Zhurong's offspring (祝融氏后裔八姓之一), moved southward from one place to another and finally settled down in Jingshan (荆山) of the present Hubei. As they had supported the State of Zhou in overthrowing the Shang rulers and in founding the Zhou Dynasty, their chieftain Yuxiong (鬻熊) became the Minister of Fire. Owing to the fact that affiliation played a part much more important than that of contributions in the enfeoffment, Yuxiong's great grandson Xiong Yi (熊绎) was only endowed the title of viscount and the scant fief of fifty *li* (about 20 square kilometers). He went in the capacity of head of the state to join in the Alliance Meeting of Qiyang (岐阳之搜) in high spirits, only to be snubbed by the royalty and the other noblemen because of his low rank, about which not a few of his successors could not help feeling indignant. King Wu (?-690 BC), seeing that there was no hope of recognition and acceptance by the Zhou Dynasty, overstepped the confinement of his authority to confer the titles of prince on his sons.

In some sense Chu was the font of Daoism. Yuxiong's Daoist philosophy sets store by humanity and underlines the dialectics of change which, consummated by such sages as Laozi (李聃, from the State of Chu), Confucius (孔丘, 551-479 BC), Zhuangzi (庄周, descendant of the royal clan of Chu, 369-286 BC) and Qu Yuan (屈原, descendant of the royal clan of Chu, appr. 340–278 BC), have evolved into Daoism and become the core of Confucianism.

What with the influence of the philosophy and what with the spur out of the discrimination on the part of the Zhou monarchs, in the early stages of the state the Chu people had constantly striven to survive and to become stronger. When describing their arduous pioneering efforts, the great historian Zuo Qiuming (左丘明) says, in his *The Spring and Autumn Annals* (《左传》), that "dressed in miserable rags and tatters they opened up wasteland with simple wooden handcarts", that King Wu of Chu "launched a great campaign to enlighten the uncivilized." The successors carried forward the strategy for development. King Zhao of Zhou (?–1002 BC) had twice led an expedition to punish Chu, and Duke Huan of the State of Qi had made war against Chu on the pretext that Chu hadn't paid due respect for the Zhou Dynasty, but they had not held back Chu's rise. In the reign of King Zhuang (?–591), Chu stunned the other states with the single feat of reforms and secured a dominant position over them. In its prime the state claimed a domain that would cover today's eleven provinces. Without a wise strategy, what's obtained today would be lost tomorrow. On the one hand, the Chu people had adapted the Central Plain culture, which they had brought along, to the situation through renovation and reformation; on the other they had taken a magnanimous attitude towards the tribes and minor nationalities that had different values, beliefs, mores and traditions, and had absorbed whatever cultural genes they deemed suitable for the circumstances. For example, their worship of fire and red had stemmed from their innate beliefs related to their ancestor Zhurong, whereas their belief in the Art of Wu (a combination of medicine, folklore, astrology and necromantic art, etc.), which was advantageous for the survival of men in perilous environments, had resulted from the integrity of the notion "unity oneness of nature and man" and the necromantic art of the Multitude of Yues (including the Jing people); and the perfect image of the Phoenix, which tallied with the tradition of most racial groups in the south and thus might favor the cultivation of cultural awareness, had been the creation in light of the idea "benevolence" and the nature of local culture. Researchers have pointed out that Chu had taken a lenient policy towards the submitted. Unlike the State of Qin, which used to have large numbers of war prisoners slaughtered, it chose to placate the subjects and preserve the ancestral temples of the defeated royalties. The following anecdotes may also shed light on the point. There's a story in *Garden of Doctrines and Theories* (《说苑》), a book written by Liu Xiang (刘向, appr. 77-6 BC), telling that when the boat-woman's song was translated into the language of Chu, the Prince of E (named Zixi), overjoyed, went over to embrace the boat-woman and put his embroidered cloak on her. The great poet Qu Yuan (a member of the royal family), who loved the culture of the Yue's, had absorbed the artistry in the Yue's folk songs for his creation. As a result of the appropriate policies, which had created a harmony favorable to social, cultural and economic developments, Chu began to thrive. For instance, when the Yangyues brought their bronze melting and manufacturing techniques to Chu, Chu's bronze industry was greatly boosted. In human history Chu was the first producer of the writing brush, the first establisher of the county as an administrative setup, and the first builder of the Great Wall. As a big state of the time, Chu boasted of its excellent literature, music and art. It's no wonder that its philosophy was comparable to that of Ancient Greece (800−146 BC) both in profundity and in speculativeness. Mr. Huang Duanyun, in his paper On the State of Chu, and Mr. Zhang Zhengming, in his book *History of the Culture of Chu*, both attribute the growth of Chu to Chu's policies of open-mindedness, leniency and magnanimity.

From what is reviewed above, we can see that the Zhou royalty's arrogance and prejudice was self-evident, and that such factors as culture, philosophy, politics and economy had brought the prosperity and growth of Chu, which in turn enabled Chu to accomplish its historical mission of cultural convergence and to play an important role in the formation of a great nation, which was to become a blessing to world peace and human civilization. Just as the divine Dragon born in the north is full of vigor and righteousness, the holy Phoenix created by the people of Chu is radiating with beauty and warmth. The happy integrity of the Phoenix and the Dragon yet to come would mark the maturity of the resplendent Chinese culture, which is characteristic of profundity, practicality, inclusiveness, unity of man and nature and dialectical change. Notwithstanding, the Chinese people must not loose sight of their cultural defects (such as the lack of masculinity), especially in the era when Neo-fascism and Hegemonism are looming large over the Pacific.

There had been friendly ties between the States of Yue

and Chu. As early as in the reign of King Kang of Chu, singers and songstresses of Yue songs had been sent to Chu for performances. The political alliance between the two states, reinforced through marriages of the royalties, had lasted long. Furthermore, exchanges in human resources had been frequent. The facts that the Chu talent, such as Ji Ni (计倪), Wen Zhong (文种), Fan Li (范蠡) and Chen Yin (陈音), had held important positions in Yue, and that the Yue talent, such as Zhuang Xi (庄舄), had rendered excellent service in Chu, may illustrate the case. All these had paved the way for the cultural convergence yet to come.

The year 306 BC witnessed the annexation of the State of Yue by the State of Chu. The convergence of the Chu and the Yue cultures had not only promoted the social, economic and cultural development of the south and ensured the inheritance and development of the Chu and the Yue cultures, but it had also proved to be of great significance to the formation and growth of a multinational country.

The Yue ancients are gone with the wind, but the culture they created have survived wars, famines and calamities. Researchers have found connections between ancient and contemporary mores. According to Zhou Chu's *Records of Mores*, the ancient Yues used to strike round plates while dancing, and offered deities or ancestors beef and pork at sacrificial ceremonies. Today the Yao and the She nationalities, regarded as Yues by the author of the book, dance and observe the rituals in the same way. (Zhu Qiufeng, 2004: 50) Identity in the music also exists among the folk songs of the regions in question. Feng Mingyang (冯明洋) points out that the mid-level tone of the folk songs of the Zhuang Nationality in Xiangzhou and Zhejiang's folk song "The Hospitable Girl" not only bear similarity in curvilinear regulation, but they are also almost identical in rhythm and pitch patterns; that similarities are also found between the songs in the Tuguai dialect, i.e. the Mulao folk songs in Luocheng of Guangxi, and the folk songs in Dinghai and Xianju of Zhejiang, and that Guangxi's songs of the Yulin Mountains and Jiangsu's Wuxian Melody are almost of the same kind in stains. (Feng Mingyang, 2006: 26) Besides, highly identical are the two versions of *Song to Gaohuang*, respectively belonging in the Volumn of Guangdong and the Volumn of Zhejiang in *Anthology of Chinese Folk Songs*, only that Guangdong's Chaozhou Strain is closer to the primitive style of the song in question. (Feng Mingyang, 2006: 332-333) When dwelling on the local coloring of the ancient songs of Ou (a branch of Yue) and of the ballads circulated at the juncture of Zhejiang and Fujian, Zhu Qiufeng (朱秋枫) summarizes their similarities as follows: the employment of supplementary words and clauses; freedom in form and sentence patterns in spite of certain metrical regulations; colorfulness in form; and natural ease and primitive simplicity in style. (Zhu Qiufeng, 2004: 242-344) As a matter of fact, those features are applicable to nearly all the folksongs of Southern China.

The Yue songs have a close relation with the folk songs of Chu. "It is the Chu culture that has exerted the most far-reaching influence on the ancient songs of Yue," Zhu Qiufeng points out, and "The ancient songs of Yue are the outcome of the long-standing convergence of the Yue and the Chu cultures." (Zhu Qiufeng, 2004: 12-13) To lay bare the interrelation, Zhu makes a comparison between the sampled lines: ①

> The answer the autumn orchids now tells:
> Green leaves match the stems of a purple hue.
> No wonder that among a hall of belles
> I alone come into Your Grace's view!
> (Song to Fate the Minor)
> Oh, what a special night tonight,
> Which witnesses this midstream float!
> Oh, what a special date today,
> When I'm grac'd to share with th' prince th' same boat!
> (The Yue's Song)

> Th' Yuan River boasts of angelicas and th' Li of
> Orchids; but alas, no word of love dare I say!
> (Song to the Ladies of the Xiang River)
> Oh, Trees cling to th' mount, and branches embrace the tree;
> I love Your Highness, but Your Highness o'erlook me!
> (The Yue's Song)

He concludes that the songs of Yue and the songs of Chu "have in common not only the syntactical structures, but also the techniques for depicting scenes and expressing feelings." He

---

① The English versions are cited respectively from *The Verse of Chu in Library of Chinese Classics* and from the present book.

furthers, by giving the case of the Soldiers' Song of Departure and Eulogy of the Martyrs of the State, that the two types in question "are even similar in style." (Zhu Qiufeng, 2004: 13)

Let's examine the following two Yue songs, which respectively circulate in Zhejiang and Guangxi:

> I, marri'd-off, regards a rainy day as clear
> Whenever for my parents' I'm happily bound.
> E'en the remotest place may appear to be near,
> And rugged trails in my eyes are but level ground!
> (Visiting with My Parents)

> For Mom my yearning's deep,
> No matter I'm walking or asleep.
> On th' road I fancy she stays the pace,
> While in bed I keep for her due place.
> (For Mom My Yearning's Deep)

Obviously they share not only thematic but also stylistic distinctions with each other, which may speak for the inherence of ancient and modern Yue songs and the interrelationship of those songs circulating in different regions.

As part of the cultural heritage of the mankind, the vivacious songs of Yue, passed on from one generation to another, reflect the customs, beliefs, philosophy, literature, social reality and cultural drifts of the south, thus they have been honored as "the archives of national mentality" and "an encyclopedia of social life." The songs of Yue, still circulating today in Zhejiang, Guangdong, Guangxi and Hunan, share the same source but boast of their own glamour and characteristics.

Extant records of the songs of Yue can be found fragmentarily in various kinds of books, e.g. *Garden of Doctrines and Theories* (《说苑》) by Liu Xiang, *Annals of the States of Wu and Yue* (《吴越春秋》) by Zhao Ye (赵晔), *Records of Mores* (《风土记》) by Zhou Chu (周处, 236-297), *The Miraculous and the Grotesque* (《搜神记》) by Gan Bao (干宝, ?-336), *The Chorography of Lin'an* (《临安地志》) by Guo Pu (郭璞, 276-324), *The Illustrious of Kuaiji* (《会稽典录》) by Yu Yu (虞预, appr. 285-340), *History of the Song in the Northern and Southern Dynasties* (《宋书》) by Shen Yue (沈约, 441-513), *History of the Qi in the Northern and Southern Dynasties* (《南齐书》) by Xiao Zixian (萧子显, 487-537), *History of the Jin Dynasty* (《晋书》) by Fang Xuanling (房玄龄, 579-648), *A Sequel to Bibliographies of Eminent Monks* (《续高僧传》) by the Buddhist Daoxuan (道宣, 593-667), etc. Some scholars of exceptional vision in the Qing Dynasty (1616-1911) began to pay attention to the collection, classification and research of the songs of Yue, and in this regard *The Folk Songs of Yue: In the Wake of the Nine Hymns* (《粤风续九》) by Wu Qi (吴淇, 1615-1675) et al. and *A Collection of Folk Songs of Yue* (《粤风》) by Li Tiaoyuan (李调元, 1734-1803) are probably pioneering works. From the twenties to the eighties of the 20th century, folklorists, musicologists and scholars in ballad studies had achieved a great deal in grassroots investigations and studies of the Yue songs. Two of the most influential works are perhaps Zhu *Qiufeng's History of Zhejiang Songs and Ballads* (《浙江歌谣源流史》) and Feng Mingyang's *The Yue Songs: A Theoretical Survey of the Local Culture of the South in Songs and Music* (《越歌——

岭南本土歌乐文化论》), both of which include adequate data and insightful viewpoints.

It is a pity that even the fragmentary English versions of the Yue songs are few, let along bilingual collections of those songs.

Culture is the soul of a nation, and a given nation's classics concurrently function as an accumulator and a conveyance of that nation's culture. The translation of our classics is of great significance to the enhancement of our cultural vitality, to the resistance against cultural hegemony and to the promotion of world peace. (Zhuo Zhenying, 2011: 6-8) As the Yue songs constitute a cultural heritage we are supposed to cherish, it is necessary to further the studies of them, to allow them a new form of life and a new space for existence by rendering them into English. It is that awareness that inspires the compilation of the present anthology, which is intended to reflect the glory of the Yue culture and silhouette the charm of the Yue songs.

A good translator of classics is supposed to have "the most sublimated benevolence as is symbolized by water, which benefits the myriad without vying for anything for itself," (Laozi, *The Tao Te Ching*) so that he will regard world peace and public interests as his sole purpose. Only then can he conduct his translation and research in the spirit of rigourousness without the slightest touch of plagiary or impetuosity. "However can we conduct anything unkind, /or practice anything that is malevolent?" (Qu Yuan, *Tales of Woe*)

A good translator of classics is also supposed to be a good thinker, whose vision and breath of mind may enable him to pave the way for the academic community and face whatever setbacks and frustrations courageously. "Now that pure and fair my inner world will remain, / What matters if I stay hungry and away pine?" (Qu Yuan, *Tales of Woe*)

Moreover, a good translator of classics is supposed to obtain the basic inter-cultural and bilingual knowledge, so that he may not commit such silly mistakes as to coin the illogical concept of "cultural classics", or to put the character "君" in the poem "Oh, Providence" into "heaven above" and render "长命无绝衰" into "Let it endure despite the fates above."

To bring out the aesthetic values of the original to the maximum, the verse translation theory of the poetic paradigm (with *The Theoretical Outline of Verse Translation* as its representative work) has been adopted as a guide, and comments and annotations, which are supposed to provide relevant background knowledge, analyze the artistic features of and clarify the references to the songs, are expected to be pertinent. As to the academic inquiries and discussions, such as those about the sex of the Yue who sang *The Yue's Song* (《越人歌》), about the interpretation of "绣被" and "不訾诟耻", etc., they are included in the Appendixes.

As the first attempt to familiarize the world with the songs in question, this anthology can offer only a bunch of flowers sampled from the blooming garden of the Yue songs, which span chronologically from the pre-Qin period to the contemporary era, with English versions, comments and annotations. Undoubtedly the samplings may be far from typical, comprehensive and representative. Such as they are, they express the sentiments of the Yues and reflect the social realities of the times.

Subjective as well as objective factors have determined the

limitations of the present anthology. Admittedly, the compiler-translator's correlative knowledge is scant. Besides, the objects of extant researches are mostly confined to ethnical and regional songs, and no complete coverage of the songs is available, let alone relevant English versions that the author might refer to. Needless to say the anthology may leave much to be desired. The compiler-translator will happily embrace criticisms from the academic circles.

The Research Center of Southern Culture, a provincial key base for philosophic and social studies, has sponsored the present research. Prof. Chen Yulan (陈玉兰), Prof. Chen Changyi (陈昌义), Prof. Chen Qiqiang (陈其强) and Prof. Zhou Lindong (周林东), as well as my colleagues at the Institute of Researches on the Translation of Classics and the leadership of the College of Foreign Languages, Zhejiang Normal University, have given me valuable supports and encouragements in the course of the research. Dr. Xu Weijie (徐微洁) has willingly lent me a helping hand in accomplishing part of the translation. Ms. Xu Xiaojuan of the Commercial Press has benefited me a lot with her conscientious work. Various websites and reference books have provided me with valuable data and information. Hereby I wish to render my heartfelt thanks to the above-mentioned friends, sources and institutions.

Zhuo Zhenying
Institute of Researches on the Translation
of Classics, Zhejiang Normal University
November 18, 2015

1. 盘古开天辟地歌

无名氏

盘古开天地，造山坡河流；
划州来住人，造海来蓄水。

盘古开天地，分山地平原；
开辟三岔路，四处有路通。

盘古开天地，造日月星辰；
因为有盘古，人才得光明。

Eulogy of Pangu for His Creation

Anonymous

Having hack'd apart Earth and sky,
Pangu starts to make slopes and streams.
He makes land where men can reside,
And creates seas where water teems.

Having hack'd apart Earth and sky,
Plains and heights Pangu does sort out.
Then he starts to blaze roads and trails,
On which people can move about.

Having hack'd apart Earth and sky,
Pangu makes th' Sun and th' Minor Light[①].
It is owing to th' great Pangu
That men have a world nice and bright!

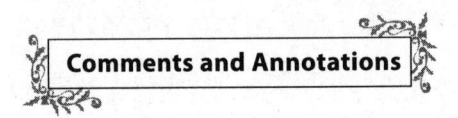

Comments and Annotations

The myth of Pangu (creator of the world), passed on orally from generation to generation, is one of antiquity. The earliest account about it is generally attributed to *Chronicle Dating from the Three Kings and the Five Emperors* (《三五历纪》), which was edited by Xu Zheng (徐整, ?-?) et al. during the period of the Three Kingdoms (220-280). Though the book is lost, extant documents with relevant citations, such as *A Categorized Anthology of Literature* (《艺文类聚》) compiled by Ouyang Xun (欧阳询, 557-641), can offer some content of the myth, which roughly goes as follows:

In the very beginning, the world was of an egg-shaped chaos, which for 18,000 years had gestated a giant to be known as Pangu. When Pangu became conscious, he found himself surrounded by total darkness, and thus he pulled down a tooth and made an ax of it. He hacked about with his ax until the chaos broke apart, when what was light floated up to be the sky and what was heavy settled down to be Earth. For another 18,000 years the sky had become very very high, the heaviness had grown very very thick, and Pangu had grown very very tall. When he passed away, his eyes, hair, blood vessels, and limbs, etc., respectively became the sun, the moon, the forests, the rivers and mountains...

Many nationalities in southern China regard Pangu as their ancestor, and there are memorial halls, memorial monuments and temples (such as the one in Guilin of Guangxi) built in commemoration of Pangu.

The present song of the Zhuang Nationality, which provides a different version of the myth, is taken from *History of the Zhuang Nationality* (《壮族通史》) compiled by Huang Xianfan (黄现璠). It narrates how Pangu creats the world and expresses people's gratitude to Pangu. The device of repetition (the first line of each stanza) serves to emphasize the glorification.

This song is arranged as the first in this book not because of its date of creation, but because of the age of the event to which it relates.

*   *   *

① The phrase "th' Minor Light" refers to the moon.

2. 高皇歌

无名氏

盘古置立三皇帝，
造天造地造世界。
造出黄河九曲水，
造出日月转东西。

造出田地分①人耕，
造出大路分人行。
造出皇帝管天下，
造出人名几样姓。

Hymn to Emperor Gaoxin

Anonymous

Having created the sky, the earth and the world,
Th' Yellow River with nine turns Pangu does design;
Ere enthroning th' Three Emperors② in succession,
He makes the sun and th' moon, which from th' east to th' west shine.

He creates farmland for growing crops of all kinds;
In order men can move about he blazes roads.
He enthrones emperors to govern the people,
And he figures out surnames as people's codes.

Comments and Annotations

This excerpt is taken from the 350th page of *History of Zhejiang Songs and Ballads* (《浙江歌谣源流史》) by Zhu Qiufeng (朱秋枫). *Hymn to Emperor Gaoxin* (高辛氏，即帝喾) is a song of the She Nationality (畲族), which narrates how Pangu creates the world and how the She Nationality is sprung from Emperor Gaoxin. The legend goes that, as the prince Longqi, the earliest ancestor of the She Nationality, was unwilling to hold any official position, Emperor Gaoxin allowed him to live around the Fenghuang Mountains of the present Chaozhou (潮州凤凰山一带).

Historical records and documents show that people of the She Nationality had suffered a great deal from the oppression and exploitation of the ruling classes in the feudal society. Early in the Tang Dynasty, they had risen in resistance. (Zhu Qiufeng, 2004: 351)

During the Ming Dynasty, some branches of the nationality moved from Fujian to Southern Zhejiang.

* * *

① In the language of the She Nationality, as well as in the Chaozhou-Shantou dialect, "分" means "给".

② The "Three Emperors" are honorable titles denoting the three distinguished chieftains of the primitive society, i.e. Fuxi (伏羲氏, God of Human Beings and Changes), Shennong (神农氏, God of Earth and Agriculture) and Xuanyuan (黄帝, Emperor Huang) rather than "emperors" in the proper sense.

3. 击壤歌

无名氏

吾日出而作，
日落而息；
凿井而饮，
耕田而食。
尧何等力？

Song of Hit-or-Miss

Anonymous

At rise of sun to tend to th' farm one goes;
His job done in th' eve, one starts to repose.
For water he has dug a well by hand,
And he makes a living by tilling th' land.
In fact nothing to Yao at all he owes!

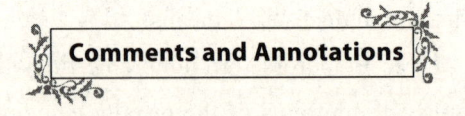

Comments and Annotations

This song is taken from *Critical Reviews of Extant Theories and Accepted Concepts* (《论衡》) written by Wang Chong (王充, appr. 27-97) of the Han Dynasty. The introduction to the event is roughly as follows: The singer, a man around fifty, was playing a game of hit-or-miss on the roadside, when a looker-on, attributing the man's idyllic life to Yao's good government, remarked that Yao was really great, on which the man replied with the song. By enumerating his daily activities, the singer comes to the conclusion that his life has nothing to do with Yao's administration. On the one hand the conclusion may sound anarchistic, on the other it expresses the singer's sense of dignity. The gist of the song is that, as the man lives by relying on himself, he owes Yao nothing at all (or: Yao's government has nothing to do with his life). The song, characteristic of natural ease, expresses the singer's self-respect and reflects the self-reliant life style of the time.

About the divergences in interpreting "壤" and "尧何等力", please refer to Appendix I: Inquiries and Discussions, No. 1.

4. 弹 歌

无名氏

断竹，续竹；
飞土，逐宍。

Song of the Catapult

Anonymous

Bend a measure of cut bamboo,
And fasten its ends with a band;
Sling a stone at th' game and chase it,
Then delicious meat is at hand!

Comments and Annotations

According to *Annals of the States of Wu and Yue* (《吴越春秋》) by Zhao Ye (赵晔), Goujian (勾践, 520-465 BC), King of the State of Yue, asked Chen Yin (陈音, a famous archer of the State of Chu) about the development of the bow and the crossbow, and the latter replied by citing the ancient poem as an explanation of the making and functioning of a catapult, from which the two weapons were developed.

The song features a style of natural ease and simplicity, and its language is succinct. In just eight characters it vividly and explicitly narrates how the catapult is made and how it works.

Another English translation available goes as follows:

> Cut the bamboo;
> Make a bow.
>
> Shoot the mud ball;
> Drive off the beasts.
> (王宏印, 2014: 3)

5. 禹上会稽

姒禹（大禹）

呜呼，洪水滔天，
下民愁悲，
上帝愈咨！
三过吾门不入，
父子道衰。
嗟嗟，不欲烦下民！

Chanting atop Mount Kuaiji

Yu the Great[①]

Alas, the devouring floods surging up to th' skies,
Driving the rank and file to absolute despair![②]
More wrathful than e'er, Heaven seems deaf to their cries![③]

Not that about family duty I won't care —
Oh, I've thrice pass'd by home without entering it —
But that with th' folk weal and woe I resolve to share![④]

Comments and Annotations

The present song was composed by Yu. In his *Records of Music: Ancient and Modern* (《古今乐录》, written in 568 AD), the author (the Buddhist Zhijiang, 释智匠) says, "In the course of taming the floods, Yu ascended Mount Kuaiji. At the sight of the rampant flood he composed the present song." The song expresses Yu's deep concern for the suffering people and utter devotion to the task.

The legend goes that in ancient times floods had often devastated the reaches of the Yellow River, and that to protect agriculture Emperor Yao (尧帝) had commissioned Gun (鲧) to tame the floods, who adopted the guideline of checking the floods with dams and consequently was banished to Mount Yushan (禹山) for his failure. Later Shun (舜), who succeeded to the throne, entrusted the mission to Gun's son Yu (禹). Yu wholeheartedly devoted himself to the cause. He dredged the streams by splitting the Dragon Gate and clearing a passage through Yique (伊阙，the gate of the Yi River) with his magic ax, invented some surveying devices and successfully accomplished the task by taking the strategy of dredging the streams. For his merits and virtues Yu has henceforth been honored as Yu the Great (大禹).

* * *

① Yu's family name is Si (姒). For his tremendous contributions in taming floods he is honored Yu the Great in history.

② The first two lines is an exclamation, in which the rhetorical device exaggeration is involved.

③ In this line personification is employed to picture natural forces. The language is plain and ungarnished.

④ It is said that Yu had been preoccupied in taming floods for thirteen years, that for three times he had passed by his own home without entering it, and that he could not even afford to spare a little time to show care and love for his baby son. As a proof of his exertion to the mission all the hair on his legs had been worn off.

6. 越人歌

无名氏

今夕何夕兮,
搴舟中流;
今日何日兮,
得与王子同舟!
蒙羞被好兮,
不訾诟耻,
心几烦而不绝兮,
得知王子!
山有木兮木有枝,
心悦君兮君不知。

The Yue's Song

Anonymous

Oh, what a special night tonight,
Which witnesses this midstream float!
Oh, what a special date today,
When I'm grac'd to share with th' prince th' same boat!①
Shy as I am, I'd boldly admit my love,
And what if people should snort and sneer?
Oh, affections well up in my heart,

Affections which are keen and sincere!
Oh, trees cling to th' mount, and branches embrace the tree;②
I love Your Highness, but Your Highness o'erlook me!

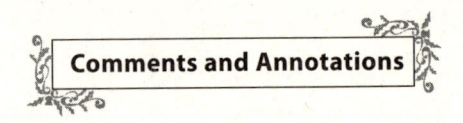

Comments and Annotations

This song is an excerpt from the 11th volume of *Garden of Doctrines and Theories* (《说苑》), a book written by Liu Xiang (刘向, appr. 77-6 BC) of the Han Dynasty, which comprises introductions and annotations to the classics that the author had collated. The song expresses the Yue's love for the Prince of E and demonstrates her courageous pursuit for it in spite of the tethers of social ethics and rites. Part of the story about the Prince of E (named Zixi, the prime minister of the State of Chu) and the Yue boat-woman goes as follows:

In the year 528 AD, the Prince of E held a grand ceremony, at which a Yue boat-woman sang him a song. As the song was sung in the boat-woman's own language, the prince didn't understand it. When it was rendered impromptu into the official language of Chu, the prince, deeply touched, stepped forward to the boat-woman, gave her an embroidered cloak and embraced her.

The transliterated version of the original is hardly understandable. According to *Garden of Doctrines and Theories* it goes as follows:

滥兮抃草滥予昌枑泽予昌州州州焉乎秦胥胥缦予乎昭澶秦踰渗惿随河湖

For the readers' information, about the interpretation of the song there exist view points different from those of the present anthology.

One of the issues is about the sex of the Yue. Some scholars insist that the Yue who sculled for the prince was of the male sex, and accordingly the song is regarded as one of homosexuality. Offered as one of the reasons is Anne Birrell's translation, in which the translator is said to explicitly allege "that the Yue's song is one of homosexual love." For information about the divergence in the sex of the Yue and in interpreting "绣被", please refer to Appendix I: Inquiries and Discussions, No. 2.

Another issue is about the interpretation of "不訾诟耻". Some scholars hold that "不訾" means "not to impose upon", and thus they paraphrase the line as "do not despise me, let alone scold me." Actually, one of the meanings of "訾" is "consider", "take into account" or "think of," which is adopted in the present book.

Accessible are four English versions of the song, which are cited below for the readers' reference:

Version 1:
What an evening is it?
I'm in a boat flowing in the river.
What day is it today?
I'm in the same boat with the prince.
I feel shy and flattered,
Not ashamed, but honored.
My heart will go on
With the prince as a friend.
Trees grow thick in the hills,

Trunks with twigs and leaves.

My love goes to the prince

But he does not know it.

(王宏印, 2014: 10-11)

Version 2:

What a fine evening this is that I've come to this ilslet midstream,

What a fine day this is that I share a boat with you, my prince!

Unworthy that I'd be so desired when have I ever felt such shame?

My heart's perplexed to no end that I've come to know you, my prince!

There are trees in the mountain and branches on trees

I yearn to please you but you do not know.

(tr. Irving Yuchen Lo, 引自马明蓉、戎林海, 2016: 59)

Version 3:

What night is this

That I steer in the mid-stream?

What day is this

That I share the boat with the lord?

So attached am I to you

That I care not the humiliation.

Eagerly I yearn

To acquaint with my lord.

Trees grow on mountains and boughs grow on trees,

But why don't you know my mind?

(汪榕培等, 2003: 14)

Version 4:

What a fine day

That I row the boat for Prince today!

What a nice night

That in midstream Prince by my side!

Low as I am

How shameful to win your love!

My heart wrenches to no end

Since I know you, my Prince!

On the hills are trees and on trees branches grow,

Longing fills my heart deep yet you do not know.

(马明蓉、戎林海, 2016: 60-61)

Version 5:

PREFACE. The ruler of Ngo kingdom in the state of Ch'u, Tzu-hsi, was travelling in a blue-plumed boat with a kingfisher awning. The Yueh oarsman fell in love with Tzu-hsi, and sang a song as he plied the oars. The ruler of Ngo was touched. Full of desire he raised his embroidered quilt and covered the boatman. His song went like this:

Tonight, what sort of night?

I tug my boat midstream.

Today, what sort of day?

I share my boat with my lord.

Though ashamed, I am loved.

Don't think of slander or disgrace!

My heart will never fail,

For I have known my lord.

On a hill is a tree, on the tree is a bough.
My heart delights in my lord, though he will never know.
(tr. Anne Birrell, 引自李贻荫, 1988: 71-72)

* * *

① These lines, which consist of two exclamations, lively convey the Yue's great delight in the event, which brings her and the prince together.

② This line presents an analogic hint, foreshadowing the idea to be expressed in the next line. The tree and its branches symbolize the close interrelation of two young people in love.

7. 渔父歌

无名氏

日月昭昭乎寝已驰，
与子期乎芦之漪。
日已夕兮，予心忧悲。
月已驰兮，何不渡为。
事寝急兮将奈何。
芦中人，芦中人，
岂非穷士乎？

Song of the Fisherman

Anonymous

Bright as they are, the sun and the moon cruise and rest;
At the reeds by the bank lies the appointed place.
The sun set, my growing worry can't be assess'd;
Now that th' moon's up, for your absence what is the case?
Not knowing what to do, I'm more and more distress'd!
Th' one behind the reeds, aren't you the desperate chase?
Th' one behind the reeds, aren't you the desperate chase?

Comments and Annotations

The present song is cited from the 37th and 38th pages of *History of Zhejiang Songs and Ballads* by Zhu Qiufeng. It is an excerpt from Zhao Ye's *Annals of the States of Wu and Yue* (《吴越春秋》). According to the book, Wu Zixu (伍子胥, 559-484 BC) fled to the State of Zheng with the crowned prince Jian (太子建) of Chu in order to prevent the persecution of the king of Chu. The State of Zheng killed the crowned prince, and Wu ran away, with soldiers chasing behind. When he got to a river, Wu requested that the fisherman send him across, which the fisherman fulfilled. Seeing that Wu was hunger-stricken, the fisherman went to get him some food. Suspecting that the fisherman might inform against him, Wu hid behind the reeds. The fisherman returned to find Wu out of sight, and so sang the song to call him out. When they got to the other bank, Wu offered his valuable sword, but the fisherman declined; Wu asked for his name, but he kept silent. Later Wu Zixu became the state's chief chancellor. He was known as a renowned strategist. The present song expresses the fisherman's worry for Wu and reflects the fisherman's devotion to the man he loves regardless of his own risk.

It is not without reason to regard the present song as one of Yue. In his *History of Zhejiang Songs and Ballads*, Zhu Qiufeng argues that the present song may be regarded as one of Chu as well as one of Wu and Yue because of the reasons stated on the book's 38th page. For information about the ground for its entry, please refer to Appendix I: Inquiries and Discussions, No. 3.

My findings might also support Qiu's argument. On a visit to Jiande (建德) of Zhejiang (October 2015), I came to the Ferry of Xu (胥口), which is said to be the place where Wu had been sent across the Fuchun River (富春江). At the ferry stands the Monument of Xujiang Ferry (胥江野渡碑), which tells of the story of Wu Zixu. In commemoration of Wu's adventure, the local people have given a nearby mountain the name of Mount Xu (胥岭), and the part of the river in question the name of the Xu Rill (胥溪). Besides, the village Qiantan (乾潭), by which Wu is said to have passed, had once been called the Village of Xu (胥村).

8. 乌鸢歌

越王夫人

仰飞鸟兮乌鸢,
凌玄虚兮翩翩。
集洲渚兮优恣,
啄虾矫翮兮云间,
任厥性兮往还。
妾无罪兮负地,
有何辜兮谴天?
飕飕独兮西往,
孰知返兮何年?
心惙惙兮若割,
泪泫泫兮双悬。

Song of the Eagles

Queen of Yue

Lo, how enviable are th' eagles[①]
Hovering in the azure skies at ease!
Now alighting on th' isles for fish and shrimps,
Now flapping to enjoy heavenly peace,
They do come down and go up as they please.
Oh, I'm not guilty of offending th' Earth

And Heaven, how come a penalty so stern?
I'm hastened north lonely with th' king;
Who knows when we'd be allow'd to return?
Alas, my tears roll down like chains of pearls[2],
And grief and cares in my aching heart burn[3]!

Comments and Annotations

This song, also entitled "Song of the Queen of Yue" (《越王夫人歌》), is taken from *Annals of the States of Wu and Yue* (《吴越春秋》). It expresses the queen's deep sorrow over the loss of her state and love for her homeland. The birds symbolize freedom, which the queen cherishes, and the rhetorical questions serve to produce an emphatic effect.

In 494 BC, the State of Yue, having been defeated by the State of Wu, had to sue for peace, and Fuchai (?–473 BC), the king of Wu, agreed under the condition that the king of Yue, Goujian (520–465 BC), should go to the capital of Wu as a hostage.

When he left for the capital of Wu, seeing that his officials were sorrow-stricken, Goujian said, "Death is what men are afraid of, and yet in my mind there's not the slightest fear of it." Saying so, he stepped on board the boat and left without looking back. The birds hovering freely overhead, the queen, leaning on the shipboard, improvised the present song.

Some people think that the birds symbolize the forces of Wu, and thus they interpret the song accordingly. A contextual survey will tell them that they are wrong — somewhere in the song the queen says "How I wish I were one of th' soaring birds!" About the formative setup of the song and the interpretation of "飞鸟", please refer to Appendix I: Inquiries and Discussions, No. 4.

*　　*　　*

① The image of the eagle symbolizes freedom.
② This clause contains the device of simile.
③ Here the word "burn" is a case of metaphor.

9. 吴王女玉歌

姬紫玉

南山有鸟,北山张罗。
鸟既高飞,罗将奈何?
意欲从君,谗言孔多。
悲结生疾,没命黄垆。
命之不造,冤如之何?

羽族之长,名为凤凰。
一日失雄,三年感伤。
虽有众鸟,不为匹双。
故见鄙姿,逢君辉光。
身远心近,何曾暂忘。

Song of the Princess of Wu

Ji Ziyu

Could one climb a tree to catch fish?
Which are known in th' river to stay?
Isn't it a whimsical act
To net a bird that's far away?
But oh, I firmly sought your love,
And 'bout rumor I didn't care.

When my sweet dream was cruelly crush'd,
My life was consum'd by despair.
When my fate went athwart my will,
'Tis no use crying o'er the spill!

Among all the species of fowls,
The phoenix is known as the Queen.
Once she loses her dear helpmate,
Her love for him will remain keen.
Though many are the pleasant birds,
None could e'er catch her eye as dear.
Likewise I show my appearance
As soon as to me you come near.
Though th' two worlds① have torn us apart,
I'll always love you from the heart!

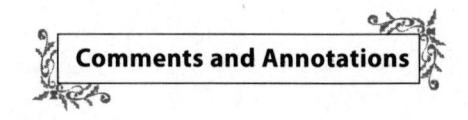

Comments and Annotations

The present song is an excerpt from *The Miraculous and the Grotesque* (《搜神记》) by Gan Bao (干宝, ?-336), which includes the romance of the the princess of Wu (Ziyu by name) and her lover Han Zhong (韩重). The first part of the romance, which may serve as an introduction to the song, may be simplified as follows:

Ziyu (紫玉), daughter of Ji Fuchai (夫差, the king of Wu, ?-473 BC), was both talented and beautiful. As she fell in love with a young man named Han Zhong, she exchanged greetings with him under the rose and pledged to marry him. Not long afterwards Han left for Qi and Lu to pursue his studies. At their son's request Han's parents went to the king to make a proposal of marriage on their son's behalf, but the proposal was furiously rejected. Consequently Ziyu died of lovesickness. Han Zhong, sorrow-stricken when he returned three years later and found out what had happened, went to Ziyu's tomb to cherish his memory of Ziyu with such sacrificial offerings as pork and joss paper. Out of Han's expectation Ziyu's soul came out sobbing from her tomb and, after imparting to him her ardent love for him and deep sorrow over the past, sang him the song.

This song expresses Ziyu's ardent love for Han Zhong and undaunted pursuit for freedom, and denounces the social system which endues parents with the right to grab their children's marriages in their own hands. The content of the song is touching, and the rhetorical devices tincture the language with force and vividness. The first four lines in the first stanza comprise two cases of analogy between the fanciful acts and the author's aborted dream for love. As a rule, the poet chooses to mention or describe something in association with what he wants to say, and the technique is called "making associations" (兴). The first six lines in the second stanza, in which the author of the song implicitly likens herself to the faithful phoenix, are metaphorical.

The authorship of the song is controversial. Some scholars hold that it is spurious, while others, such as Zhu Changwen (朱长文, 1039−1098) of the Song Dynasty, argues that it was written by Ji Ziyu before her death. In any case, the aesthetic value and social significance of the song are undeniable.

For information about relevant records, please refer to Appendix II: The Romance of Ziyu — the Princess of Wu.

*　　*　　*

① The expression "th' two worlds" refer to the world of the living and that of the dead.

10. 采葛妇歌

无名氏

葛不连蔓棻台台,
我君心苦命更之。
尝胆不苦甘如饴,
令我采葛以作丝。
饥不遑食四体疲,
女工织兮不敢迟。
弱于罗兮轻霏霏,
号缔素兮将献之。
越王悦兮忘罪除[①],
吴王欢兮飞尺书。
增封益地赐羽奇,
机杖茵褥诸侯仪。
群臣拜舞天颜舒,
我王何忧能不移?

Gathering Kudzu

Anonymous

Oh, the kudzu vines[②] are long and green,
And th' king's hate and sorrow are deep and keen.
He tastes th' gall bladder,[③] taking pain for joy;

At his word we gather hemp for decoy.
We weavers keep working hard day and night;
Of hunger and fatigue we all make light.
E'en thin gauze our kudzu cloth does outshine;
Nam'd "chisu", as a gift it's nice and fine.
Our captive king the cloth does greatly please,
And an amnesty th' Wu's monarch decrees.
Th' scepter regain'd, Yue's restor'd as a state;
The lief enlarg'd, Yue's subjects feel elate④.
Our king will surely sweep th' trouble away,
For up hill and down dale we'll with him stay!

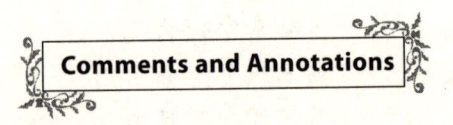

Comments and Annotations

The present song is an excerpt from *Annals of the States of Wu and Yue* (《吴越春秋》).

In his stay in Wu as a prisoner, Goujian came across an idea to win the trust of the king of Wu in order that he might be allowed to return to his own state, and thus he instructed his senior minister Wen Zhong (?−472 BC), who stayed in the lost territory taking charge of state affairs, to prepare some articles of tribute, including 100,000 rolls of kudzu cloth. The Yue women, aware of their king's plight and plan, gathered kudzu and spun and weaved with might and main.

Just as expected, when the Yues paid tribute to Wu, the king of Wu was overjoyed. In return he gave the State of Yue a scepter, had Yue's lief enlarged and conferred on Yue the title of a state, at which people in Yue felt inspired.

In 473 BC, Yue finally gained the upper hand over Wu and annexed it.

The women of Yue, who had helped their king by preparing the tribute, sang the present song to express their sympathy with their king, their joy over the successful implementation of the king's strategy and their confidence in the cause of restoration. The logical arrangement and the touching narration of the events lend the song a vivid clarity. About the background and the structuring of the song, please refer to Appendix I: Inquiries and Discussions, No. 5.

* * *

① About the content of the text and the connotation of the character "除", please refer to Appendix I: Inquiries and Discussions, No. 6.

② The cortex of the kudzu vine is rich in fibre, and cloth made of the fibre boasts of a fine texture.

③ It is said that, after his return to Yue, Goujian used to have a gall bladder hung over his bed so as to remind himself of his bitter experience and of his plan to revenge himself on Wu.

④ In poetry the word "elate" may mean "elated".

11. 军士离别词

无名氏

跦躁攉长恧兮，攉戟驭殳。
所离不降兮，以泄我王气苏。
三军一飞降兮，所向皆殂。
一士判死兮，而当百夫。
道佑有德兮，吴卒自屠①。
雪我王宿耻兮，威振八都。
军伍难更兮，势如貔狸。
行行各努力兮，于乎于乎！

The Soldiers' Pledge on Their Departure

Anonymous

With pent-up wrath and thirst for revenge,
We take up our halberds and spears.
In high morale we shall avenge
His Majesty's inflicted smears!
Like eagles swooping on the rats
Our forces will put all to rout.②
Once he becomes dauntless of death
One can wipe a hundred men out.
Providence blesses only th' just,
And th' Wu troops are inviting their doom③.

His Majesty's humiliation wip'd off,
Our army's prestige will boost and boom.
Like Pixiu, th' fierce mythical beast of prey,
We'll firmly maintain our battle array.
Let's go all out, with our courage pluck'd up!
Ho, hup — hup! Ho, hup — hup!

Comments and Annotations

Fully prepared for wreaking vengeance on the State of Wu, the State of Yue gave the former a telling blow and toppled it down in 475 BC. The soldiers of Yue sang the present song, which is an excerpt from *Annals of the States of Wu and Yue*《吴越春秋》), on their departure for the expedition. It expresses the soldiers' determination to win the victory. Cases of simile (e.g. "like eagles"), accepted sayings (e.g. "Providence blesses only the just") and oaths (e.g. "Our forces will put all to rout") make the language vivid and the style vigorous.

* * *

① 《军士离别词》乃出征前所唱。"吴卒自屠"若理解为"吴兵自相残杀",则战争犹未开始,焉知战况如何?故"自屠"当为"自取灭亡"之意,如此方合乎逻辑。

② Our forces will defeat all the enemies.

③ On its surface "自屠" in the original means "cut one another's throats," which does not make sense in the context when war has not yet begun. Hence the deep level meaning of "inviting their doom" is adopted.

12. 越人土风歌

无名氏

其山崔巍以嵯峨,
其水溢沓而扬波,
其人矗砢而英多!

The Yues' Song of Their Own Mores

Anonymous

Our mounts soar up from th' ground;
Our rivers surge along and pound!
Men are sturdy, and th' wise abound!

Comments and Annotations

This song, by glorifying the mounts and rills in the region of Yue and by eulogizing the natives' talent, expresses the pride of the Yue people.

The earliest versions of this song appeared in print successively in *Chronicles of the Three Qins* (《三秦记》, written by a scholar of the Jin Dynasty, whose surname is Xin), and *Anthology of Anecdotes and Stories* (《语林》) written by He Liangjun

(何良俊, 1506-1573). Du Wenlan (杜文澜, 1815-1881) of the Qing Dynasty gave it the title in light of *Comments on and Criticisms of Classics* (《说文长笺》) by Zhao Huanguang (赵宧光, 1559-1625).

13. 越谣歌

无名氏

卿虽乘车我戴笠,
后日相逢下车揖。
我步行,卿乘马,
后日相逢卿当下。

Ballad of the Yues

Anonymous

On sincere friendship we may henceforth count,
Thus to th' bamboo hat th' carriage is to greet.①
He who travels on horseback must dismount
And bow to th' one on foot henceforth we meet.

Comments and Annotations

The present song is cited from the 51st page of *History of Zhejiang Songs and Ballads* (《浙江歌谣源流史》) by Zhu Qiufeng. The song first appeared in *Records of Mores* 《风土记》 by Zhou Chu (周处, 236–297). It is a vow of devotion to be taken at the Yues' friend-making rite. Featuring a simple style and expressiveness involving such devices as metonymy, it vividly reflects the values of the Yues, who cherish equality, sincerity and friendship.

Records of Mores includes a brief introduction to the song, which goes as follows: The Yues are frank in nature and true to themselves. Newly-made friends are to perform a rite, at which they take the vow after dog and chicken are offered as sacrifice to the deity embodied by the altar.

*　*　*

① The bamboo hat and the carriage in this line are cases of metonymy, with the bamboo hat denoting a laborer of low social status and the carriage, a wealthy man. The connotation is that friends should respect each other regardless of the disparity in status.

14. 曹娥姑

无名氏

曹娥姑，曹娥姑，
投江去救父，
生男不如女。

What a Good Lass

Anonymous

Oh, the lass Cao E has set an example fine
By giving her own life to her father's rescue.
Oh, there are sons whom daughters as such will outshine!①

Comments and Annotations

This song is cited from the 99th page of *History of Zhejiang Songs and Ballads* (《浙江歌谣源流史》). It eulogizes Cao E for her shining example in filial piety. Cao E (曹娥, 130-143) was a girl from Shangyu (上虞), Zhejiang, who dedicated her life on the 5th of the fifth lunar month in 143 AD to the rescue of her father, who drowned in the Shun River. To cherish their memory of her, people have renamed the river as the Cao E

River and built memorial temples in her honor.

Plain as the language is and direct the style, the song helps carry on the ethics that sons and daughters should perform filial duties and be grateful to their parents.

*　　*　　*

① The comparison between a son and a daughter in the song is not meant to tarnish the male sex, but to express the idea that the female is worthy of respect.

15. 会稽童谣

无名氏

弃我戟,
捐我矛。
盗贼尽,
吏皆休。

A Children's Rhyme of Kuaiji

Anonymous

Rebels putting down th' arms,
Justice regains its charms.
People living in peace,
Officials work at ease.①

Comments and Annotations

This song is taken from the section "Biography of Zhang Ba" (《张霸传》) in *History of the Latter Han Dynasty* (《后汉书》) by Fan Ye (范晔, 398-445). The book's brief introduction to the song says, "In the middle of the Reign Yongning, Zhang Ba was appointed prefect of Kuaiji. When he arrived in Yue, he found the prefecture in chaos because of the rebellion, therefore he had notices posted to make clear the government's policy, to arouse the local people and to warn the rebels. To people's delight, he soon made the rebels surrender without resorting to arms. Hence there's the ballad in praise of him."

*   *   *

① As people live in a peaceful environment, the officials do not have to deal with serious social problems.

16. 徐圣通歌

无名氏

徐圣通，
政无双；
平刑罚，
奸宄空。

Ode to Xu Shengtong

Anonymous

Th' magistrate Xu Shengtong is just and fair,
His good government is beyond compare[1].
Between right and wrong he cuts a line clear;
In his presence sin and vice disappear.

Comments and Annotations

This song is cited from the 66th page of *History of Zhejiang Songs and Ballads* by Zhu Qiufeng. It had circulated in the central part of the present Zhejiang during the Northern and Southern Dynasties. It was first recorded in *The Illustrious of Kuaiji* (《会稽典录》) by Yu Yu (虞预, appr. 285–340). It extols Xu Shengtong, the magistrate of the Ruying County (i.e. the present Hefei) in the Jin Dynasty, for his unique government. As soon as he assumed his post, Xu Shengtong took steps to check the power and influence of the local despots, thus restoring social order and peace. For more information please refer to Zhu Qiufeng's *History of Zhejiang Songs and Ballads* (pp. 65-67).

* * *

① beyond compare: incomparable.

17. 太湖神之歌

无名氏

白露漙兮西风高,
碧波万里兮翻洪涛。
莫言天下至柔者,
载舟覆舟皆我曹!

Song of the God of the Taihu Lake

Anonymous

Th' morning dew shimmering and the west wind howling,
We rolling waves in th' limpidity howl and roar.
Though the softest in th' world, by supporting
Or turning o'er boats we oft strike people with awe!①

Comments and Annotations

This song is recorded in *Records of the Unusual*: *With Sketches* (《集异记逸文》), which is compiled by Xue Yongruo (薛用弱, ?-?) of the Tang Dynasty. The introductory remarks of the book are roughly as follows: Jiang Chen, a teacher, often goes fishing. One night, he witnessed a gathering of the water gods, at which the God of the Taihu Lake rose from his seat and sang the song while dancing. By likening the people to the waters, which are capable of supporting the boats as well as turning them over, the song offers the rulers a warning in the form of a parable that they should not be too cruel to the people, otherwise they are bound to destruction.

* * *

① Xunzi (荀子, 313-238 BC) likens the ruler to the boat and the people to waters, to which Emperor Taizong of the Tang Dynasty (唐太宗, 598-649) agrees, saying that "Waters are capable of supporting or turning over boats. The people are waters, and the monarchs, boats."

18. 咏 鹅

骆宾王

鹅，鹅，鹅，
曲项向天歌。
白毛浮绿水，
红掌拨清波。

Song to the Goose

Luo Binwang

Gaggle, gaggle, gaggle! ①
Stretching her neck skyward the goose bursts into song.
Her whitish plumes gliding o'er the limpidity,
With her pinkish feet she's proudly paddling along.②

Comments and Annotations

Luo Binwang (appr. 640-appr. 684) was one of the Four Distinguished Poets of the Tang Dynasty. His poetry is known for its vigorous style.

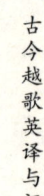

This rhyme, created by Luo Binwang when he was a little child, is on the lips of billions of children. It vividly depicts how the goose gaggles while swimming in the limpidity.

To appreciate the aesthetics of the song better, the reader may refer to the following version:

> Goose, goose and goose
> Gaggle skyward from their bent necks.
> White feathers float on green water,
> Red feet paddle and leave ripples.
>
> (郭著章, 2010: 2)

* * *

① The word "gaggle" (the mimicking of the goose's utterance) is a case of onomatopoeia, and the repetition of the word adds to the rhetorical effect of the line.

② This line involves a case of personification.

19. 杂 歌

无名氏

富贵荣华且莫求，
人凭年少作风流。
金玉满堂闲富贵，
留个声名着①后头。

One of the Mescellaneous Songs

Anonymous

One ought to strive for attainments when young,
While for wealth and power he shouldn't pine:②
Jade and gold are but superfluities,
And yet a good repute will fore'er shine!③

Comments and Annotations

This song of the Zhuang Nationality (壮族), taken from the 16th page of *The Folk Songs of Yue: In the Wake of the Nine Hymns* (《粤风续九》), expresses the singer's outlook on life, in light of which a person's value lies in his character rather than in his fortune, for the latter is evanescent and the former everlasting.

*　　*　　*

① 着：在桂、粤、闽等地某些方言中意为"在"。

② To pine for something means to long for or to hanker after it.

③ These two lines reveal how the Zhuang people make light of wealth and set store by a person's personality and character.

20. 相思曲

刘三姐

妹相思,
不作风流到几时?
只见风吹花落地,
不见风吹花上枝!

A Song of the Pursuit of Love

Liu Sanjie

I'm in love, and why not?
Why not strike while the iron is hot?
Lo, one can only see flowers blown down by th' breeze,
Whoe'er has seen th' fallen flowers brought up to th' trees?①

Comments and Annotations

Liu Sanjie, also known as Liu Sanmei (刘三妹), was a renowned songstress of the Zhuang Nationality (壮族), who is said to have lived in the Reign of Zhongzong (唐中宗) of the Tang Dynasty (618-907). For her great accomplishments she has been posthumously honored as Fairy of Songs, about whom legends abound.

The earliest records about Liu are offered in *The Encyclopedic Chorography* (《舆地纪胜》) compiled by Wang Xiangzhi (王象之, 1163-1230), a celebrated scholar from Wuzhou (婺州, the present Jinhua of Zhejiang Province). Many of Liu's songs are included in *The Folk Songs of Yue: in the Wake of the Nine Hymns* (《粤风续九》), which is compiled by Wu Qi (吴淇), Zhao Longwen (赵龙文) et al. For more information about the life and deeds of Liu Sanjie, please refer to Appendix III.

For ages Liu's songs have enriched people's life, enabled people to stay sane in face of disasters, and aroused people's resistance against suppression and exploitation. To cherish their memory of the Fairy of Songs, the people of Guangxi and Guangdong have built memorial temples in her honor, and people of the Zhuang Nationality in Guangxi observe the Festival of Songs every year on the third of the third lunar month.

The present song, taken from the 11th page of *The Folk Songs of Yue: In the Wake of the Nine Hymns*, encourages the young people to hold their fate in their own hands and to pursue their happiness while they are young.

In the old society, free love was forbidden, and it was the parents that had a say about their children's marriages. The progressive idea of the song is laudable, and equally so is its artistry. Just as is pointed out by the authors of the above-mentioned book, "it is so touchingly beautiful in language and so freshly succinct in style that the value of each word in it is worthy of a thousand tael of gold."

* * *

① These two lines constitute a case of analogy, meaning "Lost time and opportunities cannot be regained."

21. 骂财主

刘三姐

不种芝麻他吃油,
不种桑田他穿绸。
穷人血汗他喝尽,
他是人间强盗头。

Denouncing the Cruel Landlord

Liu Sanjie

Without raising silk worms why's he gorgeously dress'd?
Without growing sesame how come his fine oil?
Oh, he's ringleader of the blood-sucking gangsters,
Who have depriv'd the poor of the fruit of their toil![1]

Comments and Annotations

When Liu Sanjie's selected songs, in which the present one was included, were integrated by Qiao Yu et al. into the film *Liu Sanjie* in 1961, they made a nation-wide sensation.

This song lays bare the evil nature of the exploiting landlords by enumerating the pieces of evidence in a simple style.

* * *

① In the English version, the first two lines mean that the landlord lives on the toil of the laboring people. The last two lines answer the questions raised in the first couplet by laying bare the evil nature of the landlord. The singer aptly labels the landlord as "the ringleader of the blood-sucking gangsters", for labeling is an effective social corrective.

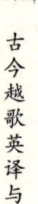

22. 财主心肠比蛇毒

刘三姐

莫夸财主家豪富,
财主心肠比蛇毒。
塘边洗手鱼也死,
路过青山树也枯。

The Rich Are Even More Poisonous than the Snake

Liu Sanjie

The rich are even more poisonous than the snake;
Except wealth and pull what have th' rich to brag about?①
Th' fish will expire if they wash their hands in the lake,
And if they pass by a hill, the trees will die out!②

Comments and Annotations

This song is Liu Sanjie's reply to the landlord's lackey, who attempts to lure Liu into reconciliation with the landlord by promises and threats.

The song expresses Liu's hatred and contempt for the rich. In feudal China, as the rich cruelly oppressed and exploited the laboring people, they had incurred people's hatred and resistance. The comparison of the rich to the snake and the exaggerations of the pernicious results of their acts lend the song vigor and vividness.

* * *

① This is a rhetorical question serving as an emphatic expression.

② Each of the clauses involves a case of exaggeration, which helps to depict the sinful nature of the exploiters.

23. 采茶歌

刘三姐

〔采茶姑娘齐唱：〕
三月鹧鸪满山游，
四月江水到处流。
采茶姑娘茶山走，
茶歌飞向白云头。

草中野兔蹿过坡，
树头画眉离了窝。
江中鲤鱼跳出水，
要听姐妹采茶歌。

采茶姐妹上茶山，
一层白云一层天；
满山茶树亲手种，
辛苦换得茶满园哟依哟。

春天采茶茶抽芽，
快趁时光掐细茶，
风吹茶树香千里，
赛过园中茉莉花哟依哟。

采茶姑娘时时忙，
早起采茶晚插秧。

早起采茶顶露水,
晚插秧苗伴月亮哟依哟。

〔刘三姐唱:〕
采茶采到茶花开,
满山接岭一片白。
蜜蜂忘记回窝去,
神仙听歌下凡来哟依哟。

Tea-Picking Song

Liu Sanjie

〔*Sing in chorus the bevy of girls:*〕
In the third month the cuckoos roam the hills,
In the fouth month up to th' brim are the rills.
To pick tea leaves the mountain slopes we throng,
Floating to th' fleecy clouds is our sweet song.

Why do th' rabbits from th' lairs run over here?
Why do th' thrushes leave th' nests to them so dear?
Why do the carbs jump up to the surface of th' rill?
Oh, it's because our songs give them a thrill!

To th' plantations we tea-picking girls go,
Treading layers of fleecy clouds bellow.
The tea bushes we personally raise,
Oho, and for our toil the harvest fairly pays.

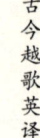

Th' tea bushes begin to burgeon in spring,
In which we pick their sprouts to make tea fine.
Far and wide tea's fragrance of th' breezes bring;
Oho, e'en the jasmine th' fragrance will outshine! ①

Leisure hours for us working girls are few;
We are to transplant rice in th' afternoon.
We pick tea leaves at dawn in spite of dew,
Oho, we transplant rice, accompanying th' moon!

〔*Sing solo Liu Sanjie:*〕
We won't stop 'fore th' flower season arrives,
When all the slopes are turned lily-white. ②
To enjoy songs th' bees will forget their hives,
Oho, and th' deities from the skies will alight.

Comments and Annotations

People, especially those of the minor nationalities in the south, sing songs while working to pluck up their spirits and drive away their fatigue, and this song is of such a kind. It expresses the girls' joy over the reaping and depicts the industry of the working people in a style flowing with ease.

In the second stanza of this song, the vivid narration of the animals' responses serves as a foil to the sweetness of the girls' songs. The third stanza expresses the joy of the girls over the rewarding harvest.

Controversially, not a few of the songs bearing the authorship of Liu are believed to be spurious, among which this is one.

* * *

① The statement that the fragrance of tea outshines the jasmine involves the device of exaggeration.
② During the flowering season all the slopes are covered with lily-white flowers.

24. 山中只见藤缠树

刘三姐

山中只见藤缠树，
世上哪见树缠藤，
青藤若是不缠树，
枉过一春又一春。

The Tree in th' Mount a Vine's Seen to Enlace

Liu Sanjie

The tree in th' mount a vine's seen to enlace,
How can th' tree be suppos'd to enwind th' vine?
If it won't cling to th' tree at a fast pace,
Year after year th' vine will regret and pine!

Comments and Annotations

This song hints that a boy should take the initiative in asking for the hand of girl he loves. By making a series of analogies it lays bare the possible consequence of inaction.

In the first couplet the vine is metaphoric of the young man, and the tree's metaphoric of the girl.

25. 竹子当收你不收

刘三姐

竹子当收你不收，
笋子当留你不留，
绣球当捡你不捡，
空留两手捡忧愁。

If Grown Bamboos You Fail in Time to Reap

Liu Sanjie

If grown bamboos you fail in time to reap,
If of good bamboo-shoots you won't take care,
If the embroider'd ball① you fail to keep,
Then empty-handed you'll sigh in despair!

Comments and Annotations

This song puts forth the suggestion to boys that in love affairs they should seize the opportunity when it offers itself.

* * *

① It is customary of some nationalities that at a singing party a girl will throw an embroidered ball prepared beforehand to the young man she loves.

26. 渔家傲

汪 东

愤气冲胸娇叱咤,
歌声如火烧林野。
皇帝低头官府怕,
淋漓骂,
直凭喉舌摧强霸。

一舸乘流风送乍,
五湖四海传歌罢。
暴力总归黄土下,
乾坤大,
至今容得刘三姐。

Pride of the Fisherman

Wang Dong

With pent-up wrath she raves, though she's of th' sex fair;
Like prairie fire① her songs resound here and there,
Striking into the emperor's heart despair,
Impassion'd and forceful, oho,
The oppressors and bullies her tongue does scare!

She sails her boat before th' wind day after day,
Transmitting her songs to th' suffering all th' way.
Those who run amuck will perish, I dare say;
As justice prevails in the world,
People are to remember Liu Sanjie for aye!②

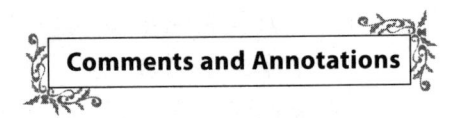

Comments and Annotations

The present *ci*-poem (词), written by Wang Dong (1890–1963), extols Liu Sanjie for her undaunted struggle against the feudal society, in which the rich and privileged wantonly run roughshod over the laboring people, and manifests the author's optimistic belief that justice will triumph over vice.

The *ci*-poetry is a verse form that had come into being in the Sui Dynasty and taken shape during the Tang Dynasty. It is also termed as "Song Words" (曲子词) or "Long-and-Short Lines" (长短句). As the names suggest, the *ci*-poetry, more often than not, is verse of uneven line length originally set to music to be sung. The music had its tune names (词牌名), and the words set to a particular tune are supposed to follow a tune pattern and rhyme scheme of their own. The tune names may be irrelevant to the themes of the *ci*-poems, as is the case with the present "Pride of the Fisherman".

* * *

①"Like prairie fire" is a device of simile, describing how widespread the songs are.

② This lines means "People will surely remember Liu Sanjie forever."

27. 吴越王还乡歌

钱 镠

三节还乡兮挂锦衣,
吴越一王驷马归。
临安道上列旌旗,
碧天明明兮爱日辉。
父老远近来相随,
家山乡眷兮会时稀。
斗牛光起兮天无欺!

Song of a Prince's Return

Qian Liu

My robe and scepters conjure a glory untold,
As Prince of Wu-Yue I ride in a carriage 'n' four①.
The sun shining in the blue skies looks like pure gold;
Flags waving on the way to Lin'an I adore.
You natives from far and wide have lent much to my awe
In the past, only th' chances for meeting you are rare.②
Oh, we've now made good what's foretold by th' Dipper's glare③!

Comments and Annotations

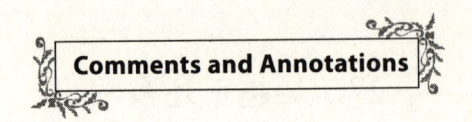

Qian Liu (钱镠, 852-932) was from Lin'an (临安) of Zhejiang. In 907 AD, he was enthroned Prince of Wu-Yue by the Founding Emperor of the Later Liang Dynasty (后梁太祖, 852-912). On the one hand he had cruelly suppressed peasants' uprisings, on the other he had safeguarded and benefited the local people in time of social upheavals by taking such steps as organizing guards, encouraging education and constructing protection embankments, etc.

After his enthronement Qian Liu returned to his hometown to offer sacrifice to his ancestors, when he held a banquet to feast his natives. At the banquet he sang the present song, which depicts the grandeur of his entourage and expresses his gratitude to and love for his countrymen.

The Shiwang Palace (侍王府), located in the ancient town of Jinhua City (金华), was once the official residence of Li Shixian (李世贤, 1834-1865), the Prince in Charge of Armed Escort. It is said that the two cypresses in the court of the palace were planted by Qian Liu, and that the prince had incurred trouble with the emblem of dragons with five-digit claws at the palace. A tourist, on his visit to the palace, composed the following poem:

> Why should mettle bring a name to the Lingyan Hall?
> For th' dragon of five-digit claws rare gifts ne'er call.
> Lo, though in a distant epoch their planter liv'd,
> Th' lush cypresses still hints at his good deeds and all!

For the author's reflections on certain issues related to the song, please refer to Appendix II, Inquiries and Discussions, No. 7.

*   *   *

① carriage'n' four: carriage with four draught animals (usually horses).

② It is a pity that the chances to meet you are rare.

③ It was believed in the old times that, when the Dipper glared, peace would prevail.

28. 婺州山中人歌

无名氏

静居青嶂里，
高啸紫烟中。
尘世连仙界，
琼田前路通。

Song of the Man in the Mounts

Anonymous

What a hearty recitation in th' purplish haze;
What a life tranquil amidst th' greenish peaks!
To th' celestial world can there be no ways?①
Lo, th' patch of field ahead for itself speaks!②

Comments and Annotations

This song is taken from *The Concealed* (《葆光录》), which includes records of weird and inexplicable events and phenomena. The author Chen Qi (陈綦), alias Longmingzi (龙明子), was a scholar of the Song Dynasty, whose biography is obscure.

The book's introduction to the song can be paraphrased as

follows: A monk from Wuzhou (婺州) went deep into the mountains. One day he met with a man riding on an ox, who sang the song, knocking on the horn with a glittering whip in his hand. The monk saluted him by making a bow, but the man rode away without a return.

The song expresses the man's satisfaction with his secluded life in the mountains.

* * *

① This is a rhetorical question that serves to give an emphatic effect. The question means there are certainly ways to the celestial world.

② Look, the patch of field ahead can give you an answer! (or: It is self-evident that the patch of field offers such a way!)

29. 月子弯弯

无名氏

月子弯弯照九州,
几家欢乐几家愁!
几家夫妇同罗帐,
多少飘零在外头。

The Crescent Moon

Anonymous

O'er the Nine Domains th' crescent moon's shedding its light[①],
In which few are cheerful but more stricken with plight.
Few can afford a marital life in th' same dome,
And more are wandering about without a home![②]

Comments and Annotations

The first couplet of this song first appeared in *Yunlu Sketches* (《云麓漫钞》) by Zhao Yanwei (赵彦卫, around 1195), magistrate of Wucheng (the present Huzhou of Zhejiang) in the Southern Song Dynasty. (朱秋枫, 2004: 153-154) In its circulation of over two hundred years, it had been developed into a four-line song in the Ming Dynasty, which is recorded in *Shuidong Diary* (《水东日记》) by Ye Sheng (叶盛). It airs people's condemnation of and grievances over the society, which deprives people of a decent life through exploitation, oppression and war, and reflects the wretchedness of people's life in social disturbances.

A different English version, which may be of help in understanding the song, goes as follows:

>The new moon shines over Cathay.
>But who are happy, who are unhappy?
>How few couples sleep together in bed,
>And many more go elsewhere, homeless!
>
>（王宏印, 2014: 112）

* * *

① The full moon embodies reunion and happiness, while the crescent moon symbolizes separation or misery.

② These lines constitute a case of parallelism, which on the one hand adds to the beauty of the language and on the other reinforces the connotations.

30. 嫁鸡随鸡

无名氏

嫁鸡随鸡，
嫁狗随狗。
嫁着狐狸满山走，
嫁着木头屈屈受。
嫁着讨饭沿村走，
嫁着流氓食拳头。
嫁着小丈夫，抱着眼泪流。
嫁着八十公公，也要好好来应酬。

Inflicted Marriages

Anonymous

Marry a cock, and like a hen you'll caw①;
And you'll become a bitch if you marry a hound②.
Married to a fool, you can just endure the sore;
Married to a fox, you'd roam from mound to mound.
Married to a beggar, you'll plead from door to door;
Married to a hooligan, you must be ready for many a pound.③
If your man's eighty, than waiting on him you mustn't ask for more;
Married to an underage boy, you must see he's safe and sound.

Comments and Annotations

In the feudal society, it was the parents and the matchmakers that determined the marriages of the girls, and consequently many women suffered all their lives. The present song, taken from the 236th page of *History of Zhejiang Songs and Ballads* (《浙江歌谣源流史》) by Zhu Qiufeng, condemns the inhumanity and irrationality of the old convention by enumerating the various cases of unhappy marriages. The style is expressively humorous, and the language is vivid.

* * *

① The use of caw is a case of onomatopoeia.

② Here "a hound" (a case of metaphor) denotes a hound-like man. The same is the case with "a fox" in the fourth line.

③ If you are married to a hooligan, who often resorts to violence, you must get prepared to sustain his blows.

31. 采桑曲

郑 震

晴采桑，雨采桑，
田头陌上家家忙。
去年养蚕十分熟，
蚕姑只着麻衣裳。

Picking Mulberry Leaves

Zheng Zhen

Braving the splashing rain, braving the burning sun,
Ev'ry family's busy picking mulberry leaves.
Why, the silk-worm raisers' jute clothes are coarsely spun,
Tho last year's cocoons were worth th' toil of countless eaves!①

Comments and Annotations

The present song is a protest against the feudal society, which deprives the laborers of a decent livelihood. The song narrates that even in a good year, the working people can hardly make ends meet.

Zheng Zhen, composer of the present song, lived in the

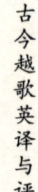

Song Dynasty. His biography is obscure.

                              *   *   *

① Though people's industry was well rewarded last year!

采桑曲

32. 树旗谣

无名氏

天高皇帝远，
民少相公多。
一日三遍打，
不反待如何？

Song of Revolt

Anonymous

Heaven's out of touch, and th' emperor far away;①
Th' officials are swarming th' depopulated state.②
Scolded and whipp'd and slash'd each and every day,
Except for revolt what could we poor folks await?③

Comments and Annotations

The cruel oppression and exploitation of the ruling class of the Yuan Dynasty had incurred the strong resistance of the working people. The present song is recorded in *Events and Anecdotes of the Past and the Present Recorded at Leasure* (《闲中今古录》), which is compiled by Huang Pu (黄溥, ?-?) of the Ming Dynasty. It reflects the cruelty of the officials and expresses people's bitter hatred for the rulers.

The song first circulated in the areas of Taizhou (台州) and Wenzhou (温州).

*　　*　　*

① This line implies that the suffering people are helpless, for there is nobody they can rely on.

② An immense officialdom, which is certainly a heavy burden on the people, always foreshadows the downfall of a government.

③ We poor folks have no way out but revolt.

33. 越 歌

宋 濂

恋郎思郎非一朝，
好似并州花剪刀。
一股在南一股北，
几时裁得合欢袍？

A Yue Song

Song Lian

Day in and day out 'tis for you I yearn and care,
For we're like th' Bingzhou scissors[①] of a perfect pair.
If one scissor stays in th' north and th' other in th' south,
When could th' happy gowns be tailor'd for us to share?[②]

Comments and Annotations

This love song reflects the girl's courage in pursuing her happiness. The language is simple but expressive, and the style features a natural ease.

The simile likening a couple of young people in love to a pair of scissors is apt, for a pair of scissors won't function properly if taken apart, besides, young girls are in general familiar with scissors.

The author Song Lian (1310-1381) was a renowned scholar of the Ming Dynasty.

*　　*　　*

① Bingzhou (并州) is the present Taiyuan of Shanxi Province. The Bingzhou scissors boast of a famous brand with a long-standing history.

② This is a rhetorical question, which expresses the girl's eagerness for the happy union.

34. 汤绍恩歌

无名氏

泰山巅，高于天；
长江水，清见底。
功名如山水，
万古留青史。

Song to Tang Shao'en

Anonymous

Like th' zenith of Mount Tai, which touches th' skies,
And the Yangtze River that's clear and pure,[①]
So unfathomable are your merits
That your glory nothing shall obscure!

Comments and Annotations

Tang Shao'en (汤绍恩) was from Sichuan. Since 1535, when he was appointed prefect of Shaoxing by the imperial court of the Ming Dynasty, he took steps to encourage education, to mitigate the rigor of government, and to relieve the sufferings of the poor. As a well-known expert in water conservancy, he had sea embankments constructed, channels dug and streams dredged to protect farm land from drought and flood. People sang the song to cherish his contributions, which appears in the 100th volume of *Collection of Poetry of the Ming Dynasty* (《明诗综》) compiled by Zhu Yizun (朱彝尊, 1629-1709). By comparing his merits and virtuous deeds to Mount Tai and the Yangtze River, the song extols the nice government of the good official in a style glowing with natural ease.

*   *   *

① In the original the case of metaphor is employed. When translated the device of simile is used owing to the consideration of cohesion.

35. 赞花瓦氏征倭

无名氏

花瓦家，
能杀倭，
腊而啖之有如蛇。

Song in Praise of Madame Wa

Anonymous

Huawa's men are staunch and stout!
Like eagles swooping on snakes,①
They wipe the Looting Dwarfs out!

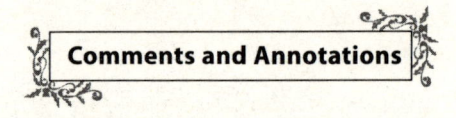

Comments and Annotations

This song is an excerpt from *Collection of Poetry of the Ming Dynasty* (《明诗综》). It sings out people's praises of Madame Wa (花瓦夫人, 1496-1555) for her heroic deeds in fighting the Looting Dwarfs (倭寇). The style is straightforward and the language is expressively succinct.

The Looting Dwarfs refer to the invaders of the 13-16 centuries who, unlike the Vikings and pirates in Europe, infested the seaside cities of China (such as Shandong, Southern Zhili,

Zhejiang, Fujian and Guangdong) and Korea in stead of snatching vessels at sea, constituting a serious threat to the local people. So far as Jiangsu and Zhejiang are concerned, tens of thousands had died in the bloody hands of the Looting Dwarfs during that period of time. At the early stage, the looters were from Japan. As they were short in stature, people called them Looting Dwarfs.

Madame Huawa was an accomplished Governor of Tianzhou, Guangxi Province, as well as a famous woman general of the Zhuang Nationality (壮族). In answer to the call of the imperial court of the Ming Dynasty, she led an army of 6,800 men to the Jinshan Post of Zhejiang to resist the invasions in 1554, i.e. the 34th year in the Reign of Jiajing. In the battles the forces under her command had wiped out more than 4,000 invaders.

After consulting my friend Prof. Lu Yong, who is from Tianyang, Guangxi, I came to know that Madame Wa's autonym is Cen Shihua (岑氏花), of which the personal name "hua" (花) was pronounced as "wa" (瓦) in the local dialect and then mistaken for her surname. As it has been sanctioned by long usage, the appellation "Madame Wa" is adopted in the present book.

The proper name of the heroine "花瓦夫人" had been a myth to many, including me, the author. About inquiries into the issue please refer to Appendix I: Inquiries and Discussions, No. 8.

* * *

① This is a case of simile, which likens the men under the lady's command to eagles and the Looting Dwarfs to snakes.

36. 送别歌

无名氏

〔女唱:〕
阿妹送郎去远征,千叮万嘱要记清。
晚上莫忘把被盖,日里莫忘扎头巾。
〔男唱:〕
阿哥出门去远征,阿妹在家要放心。
瓦氏叫人把被盖,日里又叫扎头巾。

Antiphonal about Madame Wa

Anonymous

〔*Female Voice:*〕
As your sweetheart I send you off for th' fight,
Hoping that you'll remember what I say:
Keep warm with th' cotton-padded quilt at night,
And tie the towel round your head[①] by day!
〔*Male Voice:*〕
For th' expedition I will soon set out,
Hoping you'll at home set your heart at rest:
Madame Wa will see our life's car'd about,
For her kind-heartedness has stood the test.

Comments and Annotations

This is an antiphonal of the Zhuang Nationality sung at the departure of the man. At first it circulated in Guangxi and then was brought by the soldiers to the battle fronts in Jiangsu, Zhejiang and Korea during the Ming Dynasty. By relating to such seemingly trivial details as keeping warm with quilts and towels, the antiphonal gives expression to the deep love between the lover and his sweetheart (or between the husband and wife) and eulogizes the meticulous care of Madame Wa for the soldiers who follow her to the places mentioned above to fight the Looting Dwarfs. According to relevant records, Madame Wa showed great concern for her soldiers. In case her army was in lack of food, she would allow the soldiers to go hunting at the intervals of battles. For information about Madame Wa and the Looting Dwarfs, the reader may refer to the notes of the preceding song.

* * *

① It is customary of the Zhuang Nationality for a man to tie a towel round his head.

37. 重 逢(节选)

无名氏

生不丢来死不丢,
好比青藤缠石榴。
青藤缠了石榴树,
花枯藤干死不休。

Reunion (excerpt)

Anonymous

We pledge to stay together, rain or shine,
Just like the pomegranate and th' green vine,①
Which won't separate even if wither'd,
Once round each other they've chosen to twine.②

Comments and Annotations

This excerpt from *Reunion*, a love song of the Tujia Nationality (土家族) of Hunan, is taken from the 62th page of *History of Zhejiang Songs and Ballads* (《浙江歌谣源流史》) by Zhu Qiufeng.

* * *

① This line involves a case of simile, likening the lovers to the tree and the vine.

② The third and fouth lines metaphorically denote the sincerity and close relationship of the lovers.

38. 马桑树儿搭灯台

无名氏

〔男唱:〕

马桑树儿搭灯台(哟嗬),
写封的书信与(也)姐带(哟),
郎去当兵姐(也)在家(呀),
我三五两年不得来(哟),
你个儿移花别(也)处栽(哟)。

〔女唱:〕

马桑树儿搭灯台(哟嗬),
写封的书信与(也)郎带(哟),
你一年不来我一(呀)年等(啦),
你两年不来我两年挨(哟),
钥匙的不到锁(喂)不开(哟)。

Th' Masang Embraces th' Lampstand with Delight

Anonymous

〔*Male voice:*〕

Th' Masang embraces th' Lampstand[①] with delight,
And a letter to my sweetheart I write:
"You stay at home while afar I'm to fight.
As I'm unable to return in a short time,
Would th' flower be transplanted to some other clime?"[②]

[*Female Voice:*]
Th' Masang embraces th' Lampstand with delight,
And a reply to my lover I write:
"I'll wait twelve months, be you a year away;
Be you away for two, for two years faith won't stray.③
Without the key forever lock'd shall the door stay.④"

Comments and Annotations

This is one of the classics of folk songs identified as an intangible cultural heritage of China. It's a song glowing with glory. In the Ming Dynasty, under the command of the chieftain of Sangzhi (桑植), Hubei Province, thousands of soldiers of the Tujia Nationality went to Korea, Jiangsu and Zhejiang to fight the Looting Dwarfs at the call of the imperial court, during which the present song had been resounding over the battle fields, enhancing the soldiers' morale, and in modern times, numerous Tujia young men joined the Red Army for resistance against the Japanese fascists, or enlisted in the People's Liberation Army to free the nation from the reactionary rule, during which the song had encouraged the men to charge ahead for the security of their homeland.

This song constitutes a dialogue between a lover and his sweet-heart (or between man and wife). The language is metaphorically expressive, and the style is natural and pleasantly simple.

* * *

① The Masang (*Coriaria*, known to be a holy tree capable of bridging earth and Heaven) and the Lampstand (*Bothrocaryum controversum*, alias Lassy Tree) are two kinds of trees often seen to be growing side by side with interlaced branches, and thus they symbolize sincere love here.

② The "flower" and "some other clime" are cases of metaphor respectively denoting "the girl's love" and "another man".

③ These two lines, by means of repetition, emphatically mean that the girl will never change her heart, no matter how long she has to wait for her man.

④ As the lock and the key are well matched, they constitute a case of metaphor denoting the inseparability of the relationship and expressing the determination of the female part to remain faithful.

39. 官贼歌

叶子奇

解贼一金并一鼓,
迎官两鼓一声锣。
金鼓看来都一样,
官人与贼不争多。

The Robber and the Official

Ye Ziqi

A gong and a drum beat send a robber to jail,
While an official two drum beats and a gong hail.[①]
As the gong and the drum are but parts of the game,
The robber and the official are almost th' same.

Comments and Annotations

This song is taken from *The Seeds* (《草木子》) written by Ye Ziqi (叶子奇, 1327-1390), a renowned scholar of the Yuan Dynasty (1271-1368). By making a funny comparison between the robber and the official, it holds up the officialdom to ridicule, exposing the corrupted nature of the ruling class, which deprives the laboring people of their basic necessities. The composer touches a serious matter with ease, which makes the style humorous and suggestively incisive.

*   *   *

① Different rhythms were adopted on different occasions in the Yuan Dynasty. The rhythm of a gong and a drum beat signified the escort of a criminal (such as a robber), whereas that of two drum beats followed by a gong was adopted when an official arrived.

40. 喜鹊歌

胡 温

闽山喜鹊少，
越山喜鹊多。
如何不归去，
其奈罗网何。

Song of the Magpie

Hu Wen

My fellow magpies in th' Yue mounts abound,
Whereas those in the mounts of Min are scarce.
Why then, am I not on my way home-bound?
Alas, I'm afraid of the nets and snares①.

Comments and Annotations

  This song is an excerpt from *Collection of Poetry of the Ming Dynasty* (《明诗综》). In the form of a dialogue between two birds, the song vividly expresses the composer's deep love for his fellow townsmen and homeland, and vents his indignant protest against the reality that deprives him of his freedom. The style is metaphoric and the language vernacular.

According to *Collection of Poetry of the Ming Dynasty*, Hu Wen, a native of Shaoxing, Zhejiang, was a talented man with a peculiar personality. He paid little attention to social etiquettes. For instance, before a banquet began, he would helped himself to wine and dishes without being urged, and after he satisfied himself, he just dropped down his cup and left without bidding farewell to the host and the other guests.

When he was leaving for his hometown, Hu Wen was thwarted by the border guards. After singing the song, he fell down dead. In his baggage there was nothing but an ink-slab.

*　*　*

① The phrase "nets and snares" is a case of metaphor denoting the shackles of the society, which constitute a threat to the author's freedom of movement.

41. 职方贱如狗

无名氏

职方贱如狗，
都督满街走。
宰相只要钱，
天子但呷酒。

As Dogs Army Inspectors Are as Cheap

Anonymous

As dogs army inspectors are as cheap;
On the streets are commanders heap on heap.①
Just for gold does the prime minister pine,
And th' divine ruler indulges in wine.

Comments and Annotations

This song, circulated in the Reign Hongguang (弘光) of the Ming Dynasty, is a scorching satire on the corrupted empire. It lays bare the facts that the prime minister Ma Shiying (马士英) had gone so far as to sell official positions for money and barter ranks for wealth, as a result of which the officialdom, with numerous superfluous officials, were greatly enlarged, and that the emperor Zhu Yousong (朱由崧), who had been enthroned by Ma, was so fatuous as to indulge in wine.

In "The Biography of the Crafty Prime Minister Ma Shiying" of *History of the Ming Dynasty* (《明史》), only the first couplet is recorded, probably for the sake of avoiding the taboo of defaming the Son of Heaven (the emperor). The present original version is quoted from the 131st page of *History of Zhejiang Songs and Ballads* by Zhu Qiufeng.

* * *

① These lines, which contain a case of simile ("… as cheap as dogs") and a device of exaggeration ("… heap on heap"), exposes the evil practice of selling official positions and vividly describes how serious the case is. The connotation of these lines is that inspectors and commanders are numerous as a result of selling the posts in large numbers.

42. 怨天歌

无名氏

天老爷，你年纪大，
耳又聋来眼又花。
你看不见人，听不见话。
杀人放火的享着荣华，
吃素看经的活人饿杀。
老天爷，你不会做天，
你塌了吧！
你不会做天，
你塌了吧！

Grievance Against Heaven

Anonymous

Oh, Heaven, deaf and poor-sighted,
You have been in senile decay.
You can not see what people do,
Nor can you hear what people say.
In your presence arsonists and homicides thrive,
While Buddhists[①] struggle in deep water to survive.
Alas, as you are not worth your salt[②],
Collapse you may!

Oh, Heaven, as you aren't worth your salt,
Collapse you may!

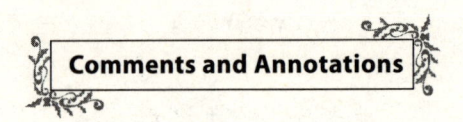

Comments and Annotations

The present song is taken from *Chitchat under the Bean Trellises* (《豆棚闲话》), a collection of stories written by Aina the Recluse (艾衲居士) of the early Qing Dynasty, whose life and real name remain unknown. The song expresses people's disgust and hatred for "Heaven", which is symbolic of the corrupted ruling clique.

* * *

① The word "Buddhists", being a case of synecdoche (提喻), denotes the honest and kind-hearted people.
② To be worth one's salt means to be competent.

43. 天上星多月不明

无名氏

天上星多月不明，
地上坑多路不平；
河中鱼多搅浊水，
世上官多不太平！

Too Many Stars in the Sky Will Tarnish the Moon

Anonymous

Too many stars in the sky will tarnish the moon;
Too many pits on the road create ruggedness.
Too many fish in th' river trouble th' water soon;
Too many officials in th' world bring restlessness!

Comments and Annotations

The present song is taken from *Chitchat under the Bean Trellis* (《豆棚闲话》), a collection of stories written by Aina the Recluse (艾衲居士) of the early Qing Dynasty.

The language is vernacular, and the song is flowing with natural ease. A series of analogies reveal the truth that the enormity of officialdom, in which lies the cause for corruption, is the bane of social evils. In the last line lies the central idea of the song, the idea that many political and social problems have stemmed from the enormity of officialdom.

Another English version goes as follows:

> Too many stars dim the moon,
> Too many pits damage the road,
> Too many fishes pollute the river,
> And too many officials corrupt the state.
>
> (王宏印, 2014: 49)

44. 长毛到西兴

无名氏

长毛到西兴，
债务都零清；
长毛到西兴，
光棍好成亲。

The Long-hair'd Having Come to Xixing

Anonymous

The Long-hair'd having come to Xixing[①],
No usury or debt needs to be paid;[②]
The Long-hair'd having come to Xixing,
Paupers' weddings are no longer delay'd.[③]

Comments and Annotations

The present song is taken from the 21st page of *Zhejiang Ballads of the Taiping Heavenly Kingdom* (《太平天国浙江歌谣选》). It expresses the common folk's gratitude for the Taiping Heavenly Kingdom, which has brought them peace and happiness.

Since the Opium Wars (1840-1842; 1856-1860), China

had been reduced to a semi-colonial and semi-feudal society. By hook or by crook the foreign powers had extorted immense benefits and snatched over 15,000,000 square kilometers of territory from the Qing Dynasty. To pay reparations designated by such unequal treaties as *The Treaty of Nanjing* (《南京条约》), *The Treaty of Beijing* (《北京条约》), *The Treaty of Tianjin* (《天津条约》), etc., the Qing Dynasty began to levy exorbitant taxes, which drove the calamity-ridden people into rebellion. The Taiping Heavenly Kingdom (1851-1864) initiated by Hong Xiuquan (1814-1864), which is regarded by some people as a bourgeois democratic revolution, was one of the large-scale revolts.

The Heavenly Kingdom's guiding principle is the concept of equality, in light of which land ownership is to be reshaped, women are to enjoy equal rights, and dictatorship should be uprooted.

As the royalty of the Qing Dynasty were of the Man Nationality (满族), which was customary for men to have the front part of their hair shaved and have the rest of their hair braided, they had ordered people of the other nationalities to follow suit, otherwise they would be severely punished. The "Long-haired", i.e. the insurgents of the Taiping Heavenly Kingdom, wore long hair as a sign of revolt, hence the term.

* * *

① Xixing lies to the northwest of Xiaoshan (萧山), Zhejiang Province.

② As coined debts and man-eating usury are nullified, the folks are thus liberated from the inflicted burdens.

③ In the old society, people could hardly make ends meet, and not a few men remained bachelors all their lives.

45. 诸暨何文庆

无名氏

诸暨何文庆,
眼睛似铜铃,
眉毛似杠秤,
起腿八百斤,
攻下麻雀岭,
从此天下立功名。

Eulogy of He Wenqing

Anonymous

He Wenqing, what a warrior you are!
Your eyebrows can compare to the rainbow,
And your shining eyes are brighter than th' star!①

You've redounded greatly to th' sacred cause
By capturing th' Sparrow Bridge at one go.
You are a mighty man with great resource!

Comments and Annotations

The present song is taken from the 43rd page of *Zhejiang Ballads of the Taiping Heavenly Kingdom* (《太平天国浙江歌谣选》).

He Wenqing (1812–1863), who was from Zhuji of Zhejiang, was a renowned general of the Taiping Heavenly Kingdom. The army under his command had successively captured such areas as Pujiang (浦江), Zhuji (诸暨), Xiaoshan (萧山), Shaoxing (绍兴), Shengzhou (嵊州), Xinchang (新昌), Shangyu (上虞), Yuyao (余姚), Cixi (慈溪), Zhenhai (镇海) and Ningbo (宁波).

The song eulogizes He Wenqing for his heroic operation of taking the enemy's vital post.

* * *

① The comparisons in the second and the third lines, which involves cases of hypobole, express people's respect and admiration for the hero.

46. 宝刀歌

无名氏

我有宝刀真利市,
快活沙场死!
短衣匹马出都门,
喇叭铜鼓声!
赴战地,临大敌,
战袍滴滴胡儿血。
自问平生,博得自由,
头颅一掷轻!

Song of the Sword

Anonymous

I have a sword that's nice and sharp,
With which I will fight to reshape our fate.
The militant bugle and drum resounding,
On horseback I gallop out of the city gate!
We'll glorify our uniforms with the alien's[①] blood;
We'll go to the battle fields to confront the foes!
For freedom's sake we'll willingly dedicate our lives,
And we're prepared to deal the corrupted head-on blows!

Comments and Annotations

The present song is taken from the 141st page of Zhu Qiufeng's *History of Zhejiang Songs and Ballads*. To overthrow the Qing rulers, an institute for military training was established in the name of the Datong Teachers' Academy by Xu Xilin (徐锡麟, 1873-1907), Tao Chengzhang (陶成章, 1878-1912), Qiu Jin (秋瑾, 1875-1907), Zhu Shaokang (竺绍康, 1877-1910) and other revolutionaries. The academy had nurtured a number of talented personnel for the Xinhai National Revolution (辛亥革命), an epoch-making event. In 1911, the Xinhai National Revolution toppled down the Qing Dynasty and established the National Government, thus putting an end to the rotten feudal society.

The present school song of the academy calls on people to rise in resistance and encourages them to fight for freedom at any cost.

* * *

① Here "the alien" refers to the ruling class of the Qing Dynasty and the invaders who ride roughshod over the Chinese people.

47. 嵊县有个牛大王

无名氏

闯闯闯闯又闯闯，
嵊县有个牛大王。
安乐财主勿要当，
百亩良田都卖光。
募捐买枪闹革命，
组织一个平阳党。
反清灭洋救中国，
联络好汉徐、秋、王。

Our Hero from th' Sheng County

Anonymous

Revolt, revolt, revolt! Rise in revolt!
The lead our hero from th' Sheng County takes!
Having sold out his fortune and estates,
Th' status as a rich man he thus forsakes.
He's set up th' Pingyang Party, and the funds
He's rais'd for the revolution abound.
To purge China of the evil forces[①],
He has Xu, Qiu, Wang[②] and others around.

Comments and Annotations

This song is taken from Zhu Qiufeng's *History of Zhejiang Songs and Ballads* (《浙江歌谣源流史》). It eulogizes the hero Zhu shaokang (竺绍康) for his heroic revolutionary activities.

* * *

① The evil forces refer to the Qing rulers and the foreign powers.

② Xu, Qiu and Wang respectively refer to Xu Xilin (徐锡麟), Qiu Jin (秋瑾) and Wang Jinfa (王金发).

48. 辛亥革命山歌

无名氏

辛亥革命来得欢,
男人辫子都剪光。
女人放脚学畲客,
原来五族都一样。
辛亥革命来得猛,
皇帝赶出紫禁城。
中国有个孙中山,
男女平等又平权。

A Folk Song of the Xinhai Revolution

Anonymous

Th' Xinhai Revolution is nice and fine,
To have men's plaits cut off 'tis is a sign.①
Equality achiev'd, gone are th' days dark,
Which th' abatement of foot-binding② does mark.
The Xinhai Revolution's shining bright,
At which th' emperor had to take to flight.
Sun Zhongshan is really China's great pride:
He enables us to be dignified!

Comments and Annotations

This song, taken from the 143th page of Zhu Qiufeng's *History of Zhejiang Songs and Ballads*, circulated in Zhejiang after the Xinhai National Revolution succeeded in 1910. It expresses people's ardent support to and hearty gratitude for the revolution, which has won equality and freedom for the oppressed.

The mention of the revolution naturally reminds people of Sun Zhongshan (孙中山, 1866–1925), alias Sun Yat-sen (孙逸仙), who was the great pioneer and leader of the Chinese bourgeois revolution as well as the founder of the Nationadist Party and Republic China. He was born in the Xiangshan County (the present Zhongshan County), Guangdong Province. Under the influence of the revolutionary tradition of Guangdong, he cherished the sacred cause of the Taiping Heavenly Kingdom when young. He set up the Chinese Revolutionary Alliance (中国同盟会) in 1905. When the Xinhai Revolution won the victory, he was elected Preliminary President of Republic China.

Sun Zhongshan's works, such as *Strategy for the Construction of the Nation* (《建国方略》), *Outline for National Construction* (《建国大纲》), *Human Rights, People's Livelihood and National Independence* (《三民主义》), etc., are included in the 11-volumn *Complete Works of Sun Zhongshan* (《孙中山全集》), which was published in 1986 by China Publishing Bureau (中华书局).

* * *

① According to the law of the Qing Dynasty, men were to wear plaits, as was customary of the Man Nationality (满族).The act of having people's plaits cut off signifies the determination to break away from the rule and convention of the Qing Dynasty.

② It was stipulated in the law of the Qing Dynasty that women should have their feet bound, which resulted in the deformity of the feet.

49. 送郎当红军

无名氏

送郎去当红军，
革命要认清，
豪绅呐地主呀，
剥削我穷人。
哎呀我的郎我的郎！
送郎去当红军，
切莫想家庭，
家中呐事务呀，
妹妹会小心。

I Send You, Darling, to the Red Army

Anonymous

I send you, darling, to the Red Army,
Hoping of th' aim of revolution you'll be aware.
It is the despots and landlords
That have driven the poor to despair.
Oh, listen, my dearest!
I send you, darling, to the Red Army,
Hoping you'll not worry 'bout any household affair.
You may just set your mind at rest,
For of things at home I'll take good care!

Comments and Annotations

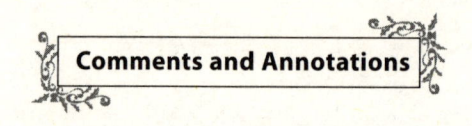

The present song, which first circulated in Jiangxi (江西), utters the encouragement and assurance of the wife (or girlfriend) to her husband (or boyfriend), who is going to join the Red Army.

The Red Army of Workers and Peasants, the Red Army for short, was an army under the leadership of the Chinese Communist Party during the Agrarian Revolution. It had a soldiery of 300,000 in its heyday. When the War in Resistance Against Japan broke out, the Communist Party and the Kuomintang reached an agreement, in light of which the main forces of the Red Army was reorganized as the Eight Route Army of the National Revolutionary Army, while those forces operating in Jiangxi, Fujian, Zhejiang, Guangdong, Guangxi, Hunan, Hubei, Henan and Anhui were reformed as the New Fourth Army.

During the Agrarian Revolution, the reforms in land ownership enabled the peasants to get back their land, which had by hook or by crook been snatched by the landlords and local despots. Aware that the Communist Party was their liberator, more and more workers and peasants joined the Red Army to fight for freedom and democracy.

50. 新四军军歌

陈毅、叶挺等

光荣北伐武昌城下，
血染着我们的姓名；
孤军奋斗罗霄山上，
继承了先烈的殊勋。
千百次抗争，风雪饥寒；
千万里转战，穷山野营。
获得丰富的斗争经验，
锻炼艰苦的牺牲精神。
为了社会幸福，
为了民族生存，
一贯坚持我们的斗争！
八省健儿汇成一道抗日的铁流，
八省健儿汇成一道抗日的铁流。
东进！东进！我们是铁的新四军！
东进，东进！我们是铁的新四军！
扬子江头淮河之滨，
任我们纵横的驰骋；
深入敌后百战百胜，
汹涌着杀敌的呼声。
要英勇冲锋、歼灭敌寇；
要大声呐喊，唤起人民。
发挥革命的优良传统，
创造现代的革命新军。

为了社会幸福，
为了民族生存，
巩固团结坚决的斗争！
抗战建国高举独立自由的旗帜，
抗战建国高举独立自由的旗帜！
前进！前进！我们是铁的新四军！
前进！前进！我们是铁的新四军！

Anthem of the New Fourth Army

Chen Yi, Ye Ting et al.

Our blood shed in Wuchang in the Northern
Expedition[①] glorifies our colors for aye;
Our struggle in the Luoxiao Mounts[②] embodies
The spirit of our martyrs brought to full play.
Countless actions 'gainst pains and rains
And countless fights 'midst many a rill and hill
Have enrich'd our experience, nurtured
Our devotion, and tempered our will!
In order that the people may thrive,
In order that our nation may survive,
We'll forever forever strive!
Oh, valiants of th' eight regions, hand in hand
Let's form an irresistible force against Japan,
March east, iron-strong soldiers of the New Fourth!
March east, iron-strong soldiers of the New Fourth!

Let's sweep across the reaches of th' Yangtze
And th' Huai River against the foes;
Like a dagger we'll cut into the rear areas
And give the invaders telling blows!
We'll charge ahead with thundering roars,
And awake the folk with the nation's deep sores.
Carrying forward the revolutionary tradition
We'll make ours an army of modern times.
For people's welfare and the nation's existence,
Let's strengthen th' unity of all the climes!
Holding high the banner of independence
And freedom, we'll drive th' foes out of our land;
Holding high the banner of independence
And freedom, we'll let our nation with dignity stand.
March ahead, invincible New Fourth Armymen!
March ahead, invincible New Fourth Armymen!

Comments and Annotations

The present *Anthem of the New Fourth Army*, composed in 1939 by the great marshal Chen Yi (陈毅, 1902-1972), the renowned General Ye Ting (叶挺, 1896-1946) et al. and set to music by the famous musician He Shide (何士德, 1910-2000), had encouraged thousands upon thousands of people to fight against the Japanese fascists during the Second World War. It manifests the dauntless spirit of the Chinese people and expresses the army's determination to free the land from claws of the invaders. The style is vigorous and the melody is touching.

Having laid hold of Korea, Mongolia and Northeast China, Japan waged the aggressive war against China in 1937 and launched the Pacific War in 1942, both being component parts of the Second World War.

For human dignity, for justice, for national existence and for world peace, the heroic Chinese people rose in resistance against the Japanese beasts. Under the leadership of the Communist Party, the Eighth Route Army and the New Fourth Army had fought heroically against the enemy. Besides, they had established anti-Japanese bases in the rear areas, such as the Northwest-Shanxi Base, the Shanxi-Chahar-Hebei Base, the Southwest-Shanxi Base, the Dongjiang-River Base, the Zhujiang-River-Delta Base and the Hainan-Island Base, etc. By 1940, the two armies had fifty thousand men, and the population of the base areas reached 100,000,000.

With the Anti-Japanese United Front formed by the Kuomintang, the Communist Party and the other social bodies as the mainstay, the Chinese people had fought shoulder to shoulder with people from such allied countries as America, the Soviet Union, Britain and Canada for eight years until they won the final victory in 1945.

* * *

① The Northern Expedition (1926–1928), with the National Revolutionary Army as the main force, purposed the unification of the nation, which had been torn to pieces by the regimes of the warlords. As the regiment under the command of General Ye Ting was one of the most heroic and combat-worthy forces, people honored it as "The Iron Regiment."

② The Luoxiao Mounts (罗霄山), where the Red Army sprang up as an invincible revolutionary armed force, are located across Hunan and Jiangxi Provinces.

51. 松竹茶山升红旗

无名氏

毛主席，在延安，
想到四明山，
派来好领导，
敌后来抗战；
组织游击队，
胜利在眼前。
松竹茶山升红旗，
百姓见青天。

Red Flags Are Waving in the Songzhu Tea Mounts

Anonymous

Though he's in Yan'an far far away,
Chairman Mao[①] has a thought for us here.
He has sent talent to the Siming Mounts[②],
So that th' invaders are fought at the rear.
Guerrillas having been organized,
The victory of resistance is near.
Red flags are waving in th' Songzhu Tea Mounts,
And in th' sunlight of justice th' folks are of good cheer!

Comments and Annotations

The present song expresses people's gratitude towards the Communist Party and Chairman Mao, as well as their determination to win the final victory. The language is vernacular and the style is simple and natural.

Since December 1937, the Communist Party and the revolutionary forces began to set up anti-Japanese bases in the enemy-occupied areas, where local governments were established, armed forces were organized, rents and interest rates were reduced. With the ardent support of the people, the armed forces effectively took steps to punish the traitors, recruit soldiers and raise military provisions.

In March 1939, Vice-chairman Zhou Enlai (1898-1976) of the Central Military Committee made an inspection tour to Shaoxing, Zhuji and Jinhua, when he gave the local party organizations instructions concerning the resistance against Japan. Later some Communists were dispatched from Shanghai to the Siming Mounts to set up a revolutionary base.

In 1941, the guerrillas under the leadership of the Shanghai Committee crossed the Hangzhou Gulf and entered Zhejiang. The next year, the Anti-Japanese Base of Eastern Zhejiang centering round the Siming Mounts was established. By the year 1945, the armed forces had been engaged in 643 battles and encounters, captured two county seats and 110 enemy posts, and liberated 4,000,000 people.

*　*　*

① Mao Zedong (1893-1976) was a great Marxist strategist, theorist and statesman, as well as a great poet and calligraphist. He had led the Chinese people in their long-term struggle for freedom and independence. As one of the founders of the people's army and the People's Republic of China, he had been Head of the State for a long period of time. His great contributions to the cause of liberation have won him the heart-felt esteem of the Chinese people, who respectfully address him Chairman Mao.

② The Siming Mounts refer to the Siming Mountain Range, which lies in the east of Zhejiang, has a floor coverage of over 6,665 hectares. Its highest peak boasts of an altitude of 1,020 meters above sea level.

52. 保卫新昌

无名氏

生新昌,长新昌,
越王的子孙不是羔羊!
背着刀,背着枪,
为了活命上战场。
来一个,杀一个,
来两个就杀一双!

In Defence of Xinchang

Anonymous

We were born in Xinchang, and we've grown up here.
As offspring of King of Yue[①] we aren't goats prone to fear[②].
Let's take up our arms and fight hand in hand,
And for existence we must defend our land.
If the woe is alone, we'll wipe out one;
And we'll wipe out a pair if two foes come![③]

Comments and Annotations

During the Second World War, the Japanese invaders had made attempts to cut off the connection between the guerrilla forces operating respectively in the Siming Mounts and in the Yandang-Kuocang area. The present song expresses the guerillas' determination to defend their base area. The style is vigorous.

* * *

① For information about the king of Yue, the reader may refer to the notes to "Song of the Catapult" and "Song of the Eagles".

② Unlike the goats, which easily get frightened, we are fearless.

③ No matter how many the enemies are, we are determined to wipe them all out!

53. 龙山中学校歌

梁荫源

龙山之阳,
东海之光,
年轻活泼的一群,
来自四方。
团结一堂,
垦此田野,
辟此山荒;
在暴风雨中成长,
在战斗中健壮。
学习工作工作学习,
民主的作风,
进步的榜样。
严肃紧张紧张严肃,
今天是抗日的先锋,
明天是建国的勇将。
是摧毁旧社会的战士,
是创造新中国的栋梁。
同学们,努力前进,
进向那革命的战场!

Anthem of Longshan Middle School

Liang Yinyuan

In th's south of th' Longshan Mountains
Is located a school as Donghai's[①] pride,
Where we vigorous youth
Gather from far and wide.
To blaze new trails and probe into new scopes
We'll take great pains;
We grow stronger and stronger,
Braving th' storms of winds and rains.
Exert ourselves in our work,
Exert ourselves in study!
We are models of progress;
We are models of democracy!
In the spirit of devotion,
In the spirit of industry,
Let's fight as today's vanguards in resisting Japan,
Let's endeavor as morrow's backbone of our country!
Fellow students, let's forge ahead!
In the name of revolution,
Let's forge ahead!

Comments and Annotations

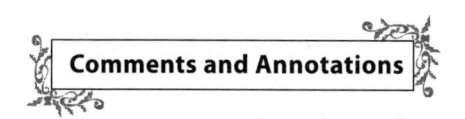

The song, composed by Liang Yinyuan (梁荫源) and set to music by Zhou Shaozhong (周少重) during the Anti-Japanese War, has encouraged the teachers and students of Longshan Middle School to strive for their nation's freedom, independence and revival. Many teachers and students joined the Dongjiang Guerrilla Column (东江游击纵队), which had been established under the leadership of the Communist Party, and went to the battle fronts to fight the invaders.

Longshan Middle School boasts a long-standing revolutionary tradition. In the Reign of Qianglong (乾隆), Chen Zhangyi (陈张翼), an official from Hangzhou, was appointed magistrate of Lufeng (陆丰) County. To encourage education he proposed the establishment of the Longshan Academy in 1737. In 1742, his proposal was materialized by his successor Chen Guanshi (陈冠世). During the Great Revolution (1924-1927) the academy was renamed as Longshan Middle School. Since its establishment the school has nurtured innumerous talent for the nation. About the tradition of the school, please refer to Appendix I: Inquiries and Discussions, No. 9.

* * *

① Donghai, situated at the foot of the Longshan Mountains, was the seat of the then Lufeng County.

54. 四明山

无名氏

四明山有多少高？
八百里方圆廿里高。
四明山有多少牢？
铜墙铁壁千万道。
四明山用啥格炮？
铁头沙子檀树炮。
四明山用啥格刀？
红布须头阔背刀。
四明山，啥格妙？
专打"皇军""和平佬"。
四明山，为谁好？
帮助穷人斗土豪。
四明山，谁领导？
共产党里有朱、毛。

Song of the Siming Mounts

Anonymous

— Do you know how big and how tall are th' Siming Mounts?
— They are scores of *li* 'round and twenty *li* in height.

— Then would you tell me how precipitous they are?
— Th' iron-like rocks and cliffs would give the foes a fright.

— Well, do people have cannons of any sort there?
— Sure, those made of ebony trunks in iron's stead.

— What other weapons do they use in the Siming Mounts?
— Oh, they use broad-back swords tassel'd with ribbons red.

— What are people good at out there in th' mounts?
— Fighting th' invaders and their lackeys in th' disguise of "peace."

— What do people in the Siming Mounts strive to do?
— To bring down local tyrants and put the poor at ease.

— People must have got wise leaders. Can you tell who?
— Yes. Among the Communists they have Mao and Zhu! ①

四明山

Comments and Annotations

The present song is taken from the 115th and 116th pages of *A Collection of Zhejiang Folk Songs* compiled by Zhu Qiufeng. In the dialogic form it narrates why and how people are fighting against the Japanese invaders. The vernacular language and the plain style had enabled it to spread far and wide.

* * *

① Mao and Zhu refer to Mao Zedong and Zhu De (1886–1976). Zhu De was a great Marxist statesman and strategist. He was one of the founding fathers of the people's army and the People's Republic of China. For information about Mao, please refer to the notes to the preceding song.

55. 共产党像亲娘

无名氏

姚江水，长又长，
比不过共产党的恩情长；
减租减息为穷人，
共产党呀像亲娘。

The Party Has Given Us Lots of Motherly Care

Anonymous

The Yaojiang River[①] is long and boundless indeed,
But to th' Communist Party's favor it doesn't compare!
Reducing th' rents and lowering th' rates for th' poor's sake,
The Party has given us a lot of motherly care![②]

Comments and Annotations

The Party organizations in the base areas mobilized the vast masses for the resistance against the Japanese fascists, in the meanwhile they took measures to improve people's livelihood, such as the reforms in land ownership, the reduction of rents and the rate of interest. Their rights safeguarded and their burdens mitigated, people were grateful to the Party. The present song, circulated in eastern Zhejiang, expresses people's gratitude to the Communist Party. The style is characteristic of natural simplicity.

* * *

① The Yaojiang River, with its source in the Siming Mounts, is a tributary of Yongjiang River (甬江). Its reaches cover an area of 1,934 square kilometers.

② The use of the modifier "motherly" forms the rhetorical device of metaphor, implying that the party is like the mother who takes good care of her children.

56. 三五支队威名扬

无名氏

三五支队威名扬，
百战百胜赛六将；
打日本好比吃便饭，
打伪军好比喝碗汤。

The Third and Fifth Detachments Are Known Far and Wide

Anonymous

The third and fifth detachments are known far and wide;
Outshining heroes of old th' sodiers are our pride.
Every now and then they put th' Japanese at stake,
And th' invaders' lackeys are but a piece of cake.[①]

Comments and Annotations

At the instruction of the Central-China Bureau of the Chinese Communist party, the Guerrilla Column for the Third War Zone was established in October 1942. It had several detachments, of which the third and the fifth were the strongest.

The present song, which is taken from the 34th page of *Selection of Revolutionary Songs of the Siming Mountains* (《四明山革命歌谣选》), eulogizes the third and fifth detachments for their great exploits and expresses people's admiration for the heroic soldiers. The language is vernacular and the style is lively and figurative.

* * *

① This clause, which involves a case of metaphor, means that the soldiers can easily defeat the lackeys of the Japanese fascists.

57. 地下无笑声

无名氏

日本鬼子凶，
反动派可恨。
天上无鸟声，
地下无笑声。

On the Earth No Laughter Can Be Heard

Anonymous

The Japanese fascists are atrocious,
And th' reactionaries[①] are ferocious,
So that in th' sky there's no tweet of a bird,
And on the earth no laughter can be heard.[②]

Comments and Annotations

This song is a condemnation of the Japanese fascists, who have turned the land to Hell.

During the Second World War, the Japanese fascists had brought the flames of war to East and Southeast Asia (including such countries and regions as China, Korea, the Philippines,

Malaysia, Burma, Laos, Vietnam, and the Pearl Harbor, etc.), inflicting upon the Asian and American people untold sufferings. So far as China is concerned, around 35,000,000 people had been killed or wounded by the Japanese beasts (including those shot, burned, poisoned, dismembered, raped and killed or raped and eaten, excluding unborn babies and those tortured to death as forced laborers); and in addition, losses of property and war expenditure had amounted to over 560,000,000,000 U.S. dollars' worth according to the exchange rate of 1945.

Statistics show that from 1937 to 1945, the Japanese had killed 202,000 civilians and maimed 142,000 in Zhejiang, some of whom were thrusted to death with bayonets or buried alive.

Thirty years ago, I visited a "Myriad-Victim Grave" in Chaoyang (潮阳), Guangdong, when I felt greatly stunned by the data of the barbarous crimes committed by the fascist brutes. Later on I came to know that there were many such graves in China, and that only the Nanjing Massacre had taken 300,000 civilian lives.

* * *

① Here "the reactionaries" denotes the traitors, the lackeys of the invaders and the puppet armies (such as the so-called Peace-Preservation Troops).

② These two lines vividly describe the consequence of the barbarous acts.

58. 浏阳河

湖南省文工团歌舞队

〔男唱:〕
浏阳河弯过了几道弯?
几十里水路到湘江?
江边有个什么县哪,
出了个什么人,
领导人民得解放(啊咿呀咿子哟)?

〔女唱:〕
浏阳河弯过了九道弯。
五十里水路到湘江。
江边有个湘潭县哪,
出了个毛主席,
领导人民得解放(啊咿呀咿子哟)!

〔齐唱:〕
浏阳河弯过了九道弯,
五十里水路到湘江。
江水滔滔流不断哪,
比不过毛主席恩情长(啊咿呀咿子哟)!

毛主席像太阳,
他指引着人民前进的方向。
我们永远跟着毛主席呀,
人民的江山万年长(啊咿呀咿子哟)!

浏阳河弯又长,
两岸的歌声响四方。
幸福歌儿唱不尽呀,
歌唱敬爱的毛主席,
心中的红太阳(啊咿呀咿子哟)!
歌唱敬爱的毛主席,
我们心中的红太阳,
红太阳!

Song of the Liuyang Rill

HAT Song and Dance Team

[*Female voice:*]

How long is the Liuyang Rill[①]? How many turns
Bring it to the Xiang Rill from its source?
What county on the river lies?
Who steps out from th' very county
To lead the people in their liberation cause?

[*Male voice:*]

The Liuyang Rill is fifty *li* long; nine turns
Bring it to the Xiang Rill from its source.
Th' Xiangtan County lies on th' river;
Chairman Mao steps out from th' county[②]
To lead the people in their liberation cause.

[*Chorus:*]

The Liuyang Rill has a fifty *li* course;

Nine turns bring it to th' Xiang Rill from th' source.

Th' boundless waters cannot compare

To Chairman Mao's favor and care!

Chairman Mao's like the sun in his stance,

Lighting the way for people's advance.

We'll follow Chairman Mao for aye,

So that th' state power in our hands will fore'er stay!

The Liuyang Rill meanders long,

On both banks are resounding our song.

Although Chairman Mao's favor

Our song can hardly impart,

We'll air our gratitude to th' Sun from our hearts' heart!

Although Chairman Mao's favor

Our song can hardly impart,

We'll air our gratitude to th' Sun from our hearts' heart!

浏阳河

Comments and Annotations

"The Liuyang Rill", a five-stanza folk song of Hunan, is a classic of folk songs. It was composed collectively by the Song and Dance Team of Hunan Art Troupe (HAT) in 1972 on the basis of the two-stanza namesake, which was created in 1951 by Xu Shuhua (徐叔华). It eulogizes Mao Zedong for his wise leadership and expresses people's heart-felt gratitude for his great contributions to people's liberation and the betterment of people's livelihood. Its loftiness in content and richness in variation (different voices), together with the colloquial language and rhetorical devices, such as simile (Chairman Mao's like the sun), metaphor (reference of Mao to the red sun) and repetition (of "The Liuyang Rill has a fifty *li* course"), etc., all lend charm to the song.

*　　*　　*

① The Liuyang Rill is a distributary of the Xiang River, on which Xiangtan is located.

② Mao Zedong was from the Xiangtan County (湘潭县, the present City of Xiangtan).

59. 洪湖水,浪打浪

梅少山、张敬安等

洪湖水呀浪呀嘛浪打浪啊,
洪湖岸边是呀嘛是家乡啊。
清早船儿去呀去撒网,
晚上回来鱼满舱。
四处野鸭和菱藕,
秋收满畈稻谷香。
人人都说天堂美,
怎比我洪湖鱼米乡。

洪湖水呀长呀嘛长又长啊,
太阳一出闪呀嘛闪金光啊。
共产党的恩情,
比那东海深;
渔民的光景,
一年更比一年强。

The Surging Waves Foam and Break

Mei Shaoshan, Zhang Jing'an et al.

Our hometown lies on th' Honghu Lake,
Where the rolling waves foam and break.

At dawn with nets we get on board;
In th' eve with fish our cabin's stored.
Autumn harvest features th' fragrance of rice,
And ducks and lotus are seen ev'rywhere.
People say that Heaven is beautiful,
But our productive homeland's 'yond compare①!

Shimmering when the sun rises,
Boundless the Honghu Lake does appear.
Oh, surpassing the East Sea in immensity
Is the great favor of the Party dear!②
Oh, how enjoyable is the fishermen's life,
Which is getting better and better year after year!

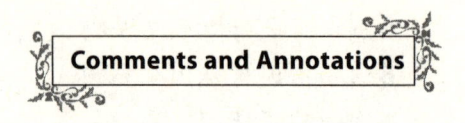

Comments and Annotations

The Honghu Lake, located in the south of Hubei Province, is one of the seven biggest lakes in China. It boasts a surface coverage of 413 square kilometers.

"The Surging Waves Foam and Break", created in 1958, is characteristic of the folk songs of Hubei in form as well as in style. The first part of the song depicts the charming scenery of the lake, and the second expresses the fishermen's gratitude towards the Party.

Owing to its exceptional aesthetic values, the song was respectively adopted as the theme song of the opera *The Red Guards of the Honghu Lake* in 1959 and of the film bearing the same name in 1961.

*　　*　　*

① 'yond compare: beyond compare.

② The inverted sentence order and the present continuous tense serve to produce an emphatic effect.

60. 毛主席，最公平

无名氏

天平不算平，
一边落雨一边晴；
爹平不算平，
欺大爱小有偏心。
毛主席，最公平，
大大小小四箩谷田一个人。

Chairman Mao Is Really Nice and Fair

Anonymous

I'd say Heaven is not enough fair,
For it is fine somewhere while 'tis rainy elsewhere.
I'd say parents are not enough fair,
For they offer the youngest child the best of care.
Oh, Chairmen Mao's really nice and fair,
Four basketfuls of acreage for each, land we share.[①]

Comments and Annotations

This song is taken from the 193rd page of *History of Zhejiang*

Songs and Ballads by Zhu Qiufeng. It expresses the heart-felt gratitude of the peasants for Chairman Mao.

Zhu's remarks on Page 193 may serve as the introduction to the song. Zhu says, "It is the thorough-going land reforms carried on in 1952 that has brought the fundamental change in the countryside of Zhejiang. Inspired by the reforms many songs in praise of the Party and Chairman Mao have been created, among which *Chairman Mao Is Really Nice and Fair* is the representative. It was sung by the old man Wang Xueyu (王学于) and recorded by Wang Wenwu (王文吾)." He adds that equality in land ownership is "an earth-shaking event for billions of Chinese peasants."

Under the wise leadership of Chairman Mao, people had not only become the masters of their nation, but they had also enjoyed an age of peace and order, when they need not close their doors at night and could always get back what they had lost, because almost everybody was honest and nobody dared to resort to cheating or stealing in that age. Nowadays people still cherish their sweet memory of that period of time, which is usually referred to as "the golden age".

* * *

① This line means to say, "Each entitled to an acreage that entails four basketfuls of rice seed, we re-distribute the land under cultivation regardless of age and sex." (Note that the local people used to measure the floor area of farm-land by the seed it needs for growing rice on it.)

61. 永远涨来永远明

无名氏

天上星，数不清，
海里水，量不尽；
海水会涨也会落，
星星忽暗又忽明。
共产党的恩情哟，
数不清来量不尽，
永远涨来永远明。

Unfathomable Are th' Waters in th' Seas

Anonymous

Unfathomable are th' waters in th' seas;
Countless are the stars in the azure skies.
The stars in th' azure skies may wax or wane,
And th' sea waters may sometimes ebb and rise.
However, never never away pine
Will the Party's uncountable favor,
And fore'er her boundless greatness will shine![1]

Comments and Annotations

This song, which first circulated in Haiyan (海盐) of Zhejiang, is taken from the 12th page of *Songs and Ballads of Zhejiang* (《浙江歌谣》, 1960). By means of comparison it eulogizes the Party's greatness and cherishes the favor of the Party.

* * *

① The last line, involving the device of metaphor, implicitly likens the Party to the sun.

永远涨来永远明

62. 十穷歌

无名氏

第一穷,渐渐穷:
终日游荡不务农;
第二穷,懒滩穷:
老孍日夜走西东;
第三穷,命里穷:
忙碌挣钱不够用;
第四穷,自弄穷:
日夜嬉赌勿做工;
第五穷,装富穷;
借债点利装门丰;
第六穷,抖气穷:
包打官司称英雄;
第七穷,拐骗穷:
终日心口不相同;
第八穷,容易穷:
勿去挣钱称道兄;
第九穷,懒惰穷:
好吃懒做山吃空;
第十穷,实在①穷:
家无柴米双手空。

Ten Causes of Poverty

Anonymous

Negligence in farming is Cause One,
Which every descent men should shun;
In idleness lies the second cause,
Which makes th' housewife frequent neighbors' doors;
The third cause is ill fate, which on one puts the heat
And leaves him unable to make ends meet[②];
Gambling constitutes Cause Four,
A habit which oft makes it too late to deplore;
In vanity lies Cause Five,
With which one will at all costs pretend to thrive;
In self-assumption the sixth does lie,
Which oft brings mishaps out of a clear sky[③];
The seventh is the practice of a fake,
Who does always his word break;
Indulgence in pleasures ranks Number Eight,
And not a few would readily jump at the bait.
In laziness lies Cause Number Nine,
With which a mount of gold might away pine;
Muddle-headedness is the last but not the least,
With which one is always with poverty seized.

Comments and Annotations

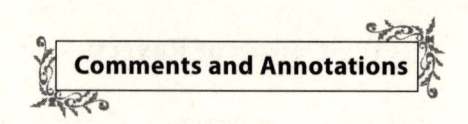

This song is taken from the 73th and 74th pages of *One Hundred Yue Songs* (《越歌百曲》) compiled by Qiu Shixiong (裘士雄). By enumerating the ten causes of poverty, it gives people warnings against such shortcomings as laziness, dishonesty, pretension and vanity, etc.

* * *

① 实在：太呆板；不会动脑筋、想办法。

② to make ends meet: to meet one's demand for basic necessities; to balance income and outcome.

③ to bring mishaps out of a clear sky: to cause mishaps all of a sudden.

63. 转娘家

无名氏

因转娘家脚头轻,
微微细雨也是晴;
远远路外也是近,
爬山过岭也是平。

Visiting with My Parents

Anonymous

I, marri'd-off, regards a rainy day as clear
Whenever for my parents' I'm happily bound.
E'en the remotest place may appear to be near,
And rugged trails in my eyes are but level ground.①

Comments and Annotations

This song is taken from the 41st page of *A Collection of Zhejiang Folk Songs* (《浙江民间歌谣散辑》) compiled by Zhu Qiufeng. By vividly portraying how happy a married-off daughter is when allowed a visit to her parent's home and how she makes light of the possible difficulties she may be confronted with on the way, it reflects women's love for their parents as well as for the place in which they had grown up.

*　　*　　*

① In these two lines, the first clause involves a case of overstatement, in which the nearness is magnified/exaggerated, while the second, an understatement, in which the difficulty in traveling is underestimated.

64. 思娘猛

无名氏

思娘猛,
行路也思睡也思。
行路思娘留半路,
睡也思娘留半床。

For Mom My Yearning's Deep

Anonymous

For Mom my yearning's deep,
No matter I'm walking or asleep.
On th' road I fancy she stays the pace,
While in bed I keep for her due place.[①]

Comments and Annotations

The present Yue song is taken from the 19th page of *The Folk Songs of Yue: In the Wake of the Nine Hymns* (《粤风续九》) in Database of Basic Chinese Classics (《中国基本古籍库》). The song expresses women's love for their mothers. It shares obvious distinctions with the previous one, which may speak for the interrelationship and inherence of ancient and modern Yue songs.

*　　*　　*

① On the road I imagine that she's walking side by side with me, whereas when sleeping I save due space for her in bed as if she were together with me.

65. 情姐下河洗衣裳

无名氏

〔男唱：〕
情姐下河哎，洗衣裳啰，
双脚跺在哟，青石上嘞哟。
手拿棒槌哎，朝天打啰，
双眼观看塞，少年郎啰喂。
棒槌打在喂，妹拇指啰，
痛就痛在哎，郎心上啰喂。

〔女唱：〕
小河流水哎，哗哗响啰，
郎影照在哟，清石上嘞哟。
妹拿棒槌哎，打衣裳啰，
水溅郎身塞，冰冰凉啰喂。
要怪就怪喂，河里浪啰，
害得情姐哟，心慌慌啰喂！

My Sweet Is Washing on the Rill

Anonymous

〔*Male voice:*〕
Kneeling on a greenish stone-board,
My sweet is washing on the rill.
As she sets her eyes on this man,

Her mindless club① gives me a thrill.
Although the club hurts my love's thumb,
With pain this heart of mine does shrill!
〔*Female voice:*〕
My lover's shadow's in th' rill cast,
With th' limpid waters gushing by.
Raising my club I knock on th' wash,
And for th' casual splash I feel shy.
Not knowing what to do, I say,
"'Tis in th' dancing waves th' cause does lie."

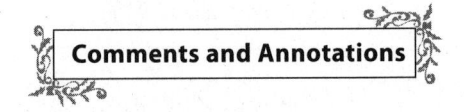

Comments and Annotations

This is a folk song of the Gelao Nationality (仡佬族). It vividly pictures the life of the young people in a simple style.

It was first sung by a peasant singer named Mao Chengxiang (毛承翔), who is from Shiqian County (石阡县), Guizhou Province. Since Mu Weiping (穆维平), a Guizhou singer, won a prize with it at the National Competition for Young Singers, the song has won national acceptance.

The employment of exclamations (such as 哎, 啰, 哟, 嘞哟, 塞, 喂 and 啰喂), which serve to mark transitions, prolonged sounds or cohesions, etc., is typical of the folk songs of Guizhou and of many other regions in the south.

* * *

① This is a case of transferred epithet (移位修饰语), meaning that the user of the club is mindless.

66. 月亮婆婆

无名氏

月亮婆婆荡一荡，
两只小狗管弄堂，
两个婆婆洗衣裳。

Granny Moon

Anonymous

Granny Moon's shimmering in th' waters — what a thrill!
Two pups are guarding th' lanes, just one of them is real[①];
Two grannies are washing, one's a shadow in th' rill.

Comments and Annotations

This song, taken from the 100th page of *History of Zhejiang Songs and Ballads* (《浙江歌谣源流史》) by Zhu Qiufeng, is a children's rhyme. As a rule children's rhymes are simple, funny, pleasant to the ear and easy to memorize. In terms of its educational function, they may acquaint children with things and nurture children's aesthetic taste, etc.

* * *

① That is to say, the other is only the shadow of the real one.

67. 呵痒

无名氏

一呵金，
二呵银，
三呵不笑是好人。

A Rhyme of Tickling

Anonymous

The first tickling means gold,
And th' second means silver;
If at th' third you still hold,[①]
You are both kind and bold.

Comments and Annotations

The present rhyme is taken from the 44th page of *One Hundred Yue Songs* (《越歌百曲》) by Qiu Shixiong.

Games help children grow up mentally and physically, and tickling is one of those games. They take turns in tickling each other to see who can stand most ticklings without bursting into laughter, and the one who's in turn will sing out the rhyme while tickling the other.

* * *

① If you can stand the third ticking and help laughing.

68. 拍拍心

无名氏

拍拍心,
囡囡勿吃惊。
拍拍胸,
囡囡勿伤风。
拍拍背,
囡囡脱脱晦。

A Ditty of Patting

Anonymous

Patting 'bout Babe's heart,
Nothing shall thee start;
Patting on Babe's chest,
No cold shall thee infest;[①]
Patting on Babe's back,
Ill luck shall ne'er thee rack![②]

Comments and Annotations

The present song is taken from the 45th page of *One Hundred Yue Songs*.

When children get startled or catch cold, the adults usually give them a few pats. Experience shows that the practice works in keeping children out of harm's way. The present ditty serves as an incantation on such occasions.

*　　*　　*

① No cold shall infest you.
② Ill luck shall never trouble you!

拍
拍
心

69. 摇，摇，摇

无名氏

摇，摇，摇，
摇到外婆桥。
外婆真要好，
买个鲤鱼烧。
头勿熟，
尾巴焦；
刮起尾巴再烧烧，
外甥吃了快点摇。

I Row, Row and Row

Anonymous

I row, row and row, ①
To my dear Granny's I go.
On seeing me Granny's in high glee,
She buys a carp and cooks it for me.
The head is found underdone,
While the tail is overdone.
So she turns it o'er and cooks it once more,
Thus I may eat it and take to the oar. ②

Comments and Annotations

This children's rhyme, originally entitled "Missing Granny" (望外婆), is taken from the 55th page of *One Hundred Yue Songs*. It is given the present name in light of its popularity.

Children's rhymes mainly aims at nurturing children's sense of rhythm and rhyme, developing children's intelligence and cultivating children's ability of speech. As is typical of children's rhymes, the present one is simple in both structure and content. However, it reflects the tradition in light of which grandmothers adore their grandchildren.

* * *

① This is a case of repetition, a rhetorical device intended for emphasis or vividness.

② Thus I may row away after eating the fish.

70. 爱拼才会赢

陈百潭

一时失志不免怨叹，
一时落魄不免胆寒。
那通失去希望，
每日醉茫茫，
无魂有体亲像稻草人。
人生可比是海上的波浪，
有时起，有时落。
好运，歹运，
总嘛爱照起工来行。
三分天注定，
七分靠打拼，
爱拼才会赢。

He Wins Who Relies on Himself and Takes Pains

Chen Baitan

Over his frustrations one may ofttimes grieve,
And dishearten'd a setback may him leave.
Sad and hopeless, he drowns his woe in drink,[①]
When a soulless straw-man he seems to be.[②]
Oh, teeming with ups and downs,

Life is like th' waves in th' vast sea.③
Be it good luck or ill luck, one ought to pluck up
And face his fate in high glee.④
As efforts rather than chance decide what one attains,
He wins who relies on himself and takes pains!
As efforts rather than chance decide what one attains,
He wins who relies on himself and takes pains!

Comments and Annotations

This is a renowned song of the Minnan dialect (闽南话), in light of which "爱" means "should" or "must", and "亲像" means "just like".

Although it is to be sung in the Minnan dialect, this song is popular even outside the Minnan sub-cultural regions. It encourages people to pluck up and strive for successes in face of difficulties and setbacks. Since it was published in 1988, the song has enjoyed a soaring popular acceptance in Taiwan and the Mainland. The last line has become a dictum on the lips of millions. The vernacular language, the rhetorical devices (such as the simile "life is like the waves in the vast sea", "a soulless straw man he seems to be", etc.), the natural style and the lofty conceptual realm have lent the song aesthetic charm.

* * *

① This is a case of metaphor.
② During which he seems to be a soulless straw man (a

case of simile).

③ This line involves a case of simile.

④ No matter it is good luck or ill luck that awaits you, you have to pluck up your spirits and confront your fate in a good mood.

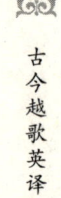

附　录
Appendixes

附录一：求索与争鸣
Appendix I: Inquiries and Discussions

其一，《击壤歌》的最早出处是王充（27—约97）所著的《论衡》，在其后的著作中出现了不同的文本。主要差异在于歌词末句，《高士传》为"帝何德于我哉"，《帝王世纪》为"帝何力于我哉"，《诗纪》为"帝力何有于我哉"，《太平御览》为"帝力于我何有哉"，《升庵诗话》为"帝与我何力哉"。本书所采用的是《论衡》所载的文本。

有学者将它归类于越歌，依据是：（1）它"首先记录、流传于古越大地"（朱秋枫，2004：1）；（2）"据音乐学家王光祈（1891—1936）考证，此歌和现代闽浙一带的畲族民歌在词句结构上完全一样（均为四字句）……它们在旋律进行上也极其相似（均多大六度跳进）音调也非常接近"（冯明洋，2006：67）；（3）冯明洋先生引用沈起炜"舜曾耕于历山，陶于河滨，渔于雷泽。南巡死于苍梧之野"（《中国历史大事年表》，第6页）一说，指出闽浙苍梧均属古越人生息之地，"虽然不能因此而断定《击壤歌》源于此地，起码可以说曾经流传于此地"（冯明洋，2006：67）。

本书认为，从歌词所带有的原始无政府主义色彩看，歌者属于方外之人或生活于王化难及的蛮夷之地的可能性确实是比较大的。兹存疑于此,以待定论。

关于此歌,拙著异于他说之处有三:

1. 有的学者认为《击壤歌》"基本上是合唱"(王宏印,2014:7),我则认为,根据《论衡》卷五"尧时五十之民击壤于途"、卷八"有年五十击壤于路者",便可断定此歌是年龄五十岁的击壤者即兴之作,是独唱。

2. 对于"击壤"的解释,有人认为是"一面干活一面用农具捣着地面"(王宏印,2014:7),这也是值得商榷的。我认为,击壤是古代的一种游戏。东汉的刘熙在其《释名》中说,"击壤,野老之戏";三国时期的吴国人盛彦在其《击壤赋》中有这样两句:"论众戏之为乐,独击壤之可娱";晋人张协《七命八首》诗中有"玄貂巷歌,黄发击壤"两句,说的是黑发的童子在巷子里歌唱,黄发的老翁在玩击壤的游戏。游戏中的"壤"最初当为土块,后来才用木头制作。关于木制的壤,三国时期魏国的邯郸淳在他的《艺经》中是这样描述的:"壤以木为之,前广后锐,长尺四,阔三寸,其形如履。"再说,《击壤歌》中老者击壤之处是道路,即《论衡》所说的"途""路"、晋人皇甫谧《高士传》所说的"道",而不是"田"或"园"。

3. 对于末句"尧何等力"的释义,一些儒家解释为"民无以名尧之德",即尧德难以言表。我认为,《论衡》在卷五、卷八都提及此事,前者旨在证明"尧时已有井矣",后者旨在驳斥"乃欲言民无能名"尧之德。"尧何等力"一句显然是击壤而歌者针对"观者"歌功颂德的驳辞:"(我自食其力,)尧对我有什么功德可言?"上文所引的"帝何德于我哉"(《高士传》)、"帝何力于我哉"(《帝王世纪》)、"帝力何有于我哉"(《诗纪》)、"帝力于我何有哉"(《太平御览》)以及"帝与我何力哉"(《升庵诗话》),皆可视作各时代著名学者对于末句的解读。

爱德华·李尔（Edward Lear，1812-1888）所写的谐趣诗（nonsense poems）比较有名，该诗体的韵式（rhyme scheme）是aabba，如：

> There was a Young Person of Ayr,
> Whose head was remarkably square:
> On the top, in fine weather,
> She wore a Gold Feather,
> Which dazzled the people of Ayr.

"击壤歌"共有五行。本书英译变通地借用了英诗的这种诗体，韵式为aabba，基本节奏为五音步抑扬格（iambic pentameter），以重构该歌的形式及音韵之美；将原作中的"吾"译为泛称代词"one"，以恰当地再现该歌思想上的普遍适用性及歌者之睿智。

兹将所能得到的几种英译引录于此，以供读者参考：

Version 1:
> We rise at sunrise,
> We rest at sunset,
> Dig wells and drink,
> Till our fields and eat;
> ——What is the strength of the emperor to us?
>
> (tr. James Legge)

Version 2:
> Sun up; work
> Sundown; to rest
> Dig well and drink of the water

Dig field; eat of the grain

Imperial power is? And to us what is it?

(tr. Ezra Pound)

Version 3:

The sun up, I work.

The sun down, I rest.

I dig a well for drink,

And I till the land for food.

What have I to do with the kingdom?

(王宏印, 2014: 7)

其二，公元前528年，在楚国鄂君子皙举办盛会期间，为鄂君驾舟的越人唱了这首歌。由于歌是用越语唱的，鄂君听不懂。有人便当场将歌词译成楚语，鄂君听后十分感动。他挥动着长长的袖子走上前去，把刺绣的背帔披到越人身上，并拥抱了她。

《说苑》记录的越语歌词是：滥兮抃草滥予昌枑泽予昌州州州焉乎秦胥胥缦予乎昭澶秦逾渗惿随河湖。

对于这首歌及其背景文字的解读，本书有三处需要特别加以说明：

1. 关于越人的性别，有人认为是男性，剑桥大学汉学家白安妮（Anne Birrell）女士在其《玉台新咏》英译本中就是根据这样的见解翻译《越人歌》的。本书不赞同这种观点。刘向根据皇家典藏和民间书籍，编著了几部著作呈献给汉成帝刘骜，是作为政治教科书用的，其中包括《说苑》。汉代独尊儒术，礼教严峻。这类典籍中不太可能公然宣扬同性恋。

2. 关于"不訾诟耻"的含义，也有多种解释，有人认为其中的"不訾"是"不加以"之意，因而将"不訾诟耻"解释为"不因为我是泛舟的身份而嫌弃我,甚至责骂我"。

《礼记·少仪》中有"不訾重器"一语,郑玄注曰:"訾,思也。"孔颖达疏曰:"重器不可思玩之,若思玩之,则憎疾己贫贱,生淫乱滥恶也。"据此,本书取其"不思",即"不考虑""不顾及"之义,因而英译时将"不訾诟耻"解释为"不顾他人取笑"。

3.《说苑》中的"于是鄂君子晳乃揄修袂,行而拥之,举绣被而覆之",有人解释为"双手扶了扶越人的双肩,又庄重地把一幅绣满美丽花纹的绸缎被面披在他身上"①。

虽然把"被"理解为"被面"者非止一人,但其正确性是值得怀疑的。首先,把被面盖在越人身上的做法并不合乎楚俗、礼仪和时宜;其次,很难想象,鄂君会滑稽地在盛会、舟游中随时准备着被面送人;再者,古代"被""服"通假。"被"有一义,指披在肩背上的服饰,读[pèi]。例如,《左传·昭公十二年》中就有两次出现"被"字:"雨雪,王皮冠,秦复陶,翠被,豹舄,执鞭以出",仆析父从","右尹子革夕,王见之,去冠被,舍鞭,与之语曰……"。著名语言学家杨伯峻(1909—1992)注曰:"被当读为帔。盖以翠毛为之。"由是观之,翠被乃是翠羽制成的背帔,"去冠被"是"脱下帽子和背帔","绣被"就是刺绣的披风或背帔,而不是"绣满美丽花纹的绸缎被面"。

"绣被"的错误解读容易引起错误的联想:绣满美丽花纹的绸缎被面——睡觉——同性恋行为。这也许是导致人们坚信《越人歌》是同性恋诗歌的原因之一。

其三,根据歌者是"楚地渔父",歌的流传区域是"吴越大地",且其形制风格与《采葛妇歌》《军士离别词》等越歌

---

① 参看百度百科"越人歌"词条。

有"前后呼应"关系等,《浙江歌谣源流史》一书的作者朱秋枫先生认为它"可称作楚歌","也可称作吴越间的古歌"(朱秋枫,2004:38)。本书认为他言之成理,予以采信。

其四,《乌鸢歌》,又称《越王夫人歌》,摘自《吴越春秋》。它采用比拟手法,以飞鸟象征自由,以修辞问句抒发越王夫人季蒬的亡国之恨和对故国的无尽思念。根据记载,"勾践临行,群臣咸哀,莫不垂泣。勾践曰:'死者,人之所畏。若孤之闻死,其于心胸中曾无怵惕。'遂登船径去,终不返顾。越王夫人顾乌鹊啄江渚之虾,飞去复来,乃据舷哭而歌之"。

当初,为了强化楚越间的同盟关系,楚昭王娶了越姬,勾践(约前520—前465年)则娶了楚国公主。公元前494年越败于吴国,被迫求和。在以勾践为人质的条件下吴国许降并撤兵。勾践在吴为奴,其夫人与他患难与共;返越之后,她节衣缩食,亲事纺织,为越国的复兴做出了贡献。

有两个问题需要加以探讨:

1. 有以乌鸢为恶鸟者,认为越王夫人是将吴国比作恶鸟,故而今译为"抬头仰望一群黑色的猛禽,狂呼乱叫着从高空中俯冲下来""那些凶恶的猛禽,已经飞回原地收拢其翅膀"[①]云云。其实不然,乌鸢这一意象象征自由,是美好的;第二首歌的歌词有"愿我身兮如鸟"一句,可见以鸟象征自由才是歌者本意。

2.《吴越春秋》载有越王夫人歌两首,第一首11行,第二首20行。有些网站及文本往往将二者并成一首,这是不妥当的。若仔细加以分析,就可明白二者并非在同一场合所唱:

1)即兴吟诗赋歌,如《荆轲歌》(《渡易水歌》)、《大风

---

① 见百度百科"乌鸢歌"词条。

歌》、《吴越王还乡歌》、《登幽州台歌》等,往往言简意赅,鲜有作如此长篇演唱者,且越王夫人匆匆随夫北行,作此长歌,也不合乎常情、语境和歌唱者及聆听者的心境。

2)第二首歌之前有"又哀今曰"的注释,而"今"与"昔"是相对而言的,可见二者的时间、场合不一,前首乃"昔日"(即离越赴吴之时)所唱;歌后又载有"越王闻夫人怨歌,心中内恸,乃曰:'孤何忧?吾之六翮备矣'",这说明,唱第二首的时间是在为奴期间、复国的条件基本具备之后;"岁遥遥兮难极,冤悲痛兮心恻。肠千结兮服膺,于乎哀兮忘食"等歌词的大意是说"度日如年,含悲受辱,寝食难安",这也可印证,第二首应是有了在吴为奴的经历之后所作。

3)从两首歌词有关鸟、虾的内容看,若并为一首,则产生多处赘余与重复,不合乎歌者的才情。

因为第二首的歌词有助于理解本书所收录的《越王夫人歌》,特将其置于此处,以供参考:

> 彼飞鸟兮鸢乌,已回翔兮翕苏。
> 心在专兮素虾,何居食兮江湖?
> 徊复翔兮游扬,去复返兮于乎!
> 始事君兮去家,终我命兮君都。
> 终来遇兮何辜,离我国兮去吴。
> 妻衣褐兮为婢,夫去冕兮为奴。
> 岁遥遥兮难极,冤悲痛兮心恻。
> 肠千结兮服膺,于乎哀兮忘食。
> 愿我身兮如鸟,身翱翔兮矫翼。
> 去我国兮心摇,情愤惋兮谁识?

其五,《采葛妇歌》选自《中国基本古籍库》之《吴越春秋》(明古今逸史本)第48页。

1. 关于歌词,本书采信明古今逸史本在其疏注中的"缺文"之说,故本书的歌词中有"饥不遑食四体疲"一句。也有误将此句置于末行的,并不成立。为了读者辨析,兹将原文文字替换为简化字,加了标点,并将其中的疏注置于括号之内,以小号字体予以呈现:

吴王得葛布之献,乃复增越之封,赐羽毛之饰、机杖、诸侯之服,越国大悦。采葛之妇伤越王用心之苦,乃作苦之诗(《事类赋》引《吴越春秋》曰"乃作若何之歌",《会稽赋》注亦引此书曰:"乃作何苦之诗"),曰:"葛不连蔓棻台台(音贻),我君心苦命更之。尝胆不苦甘如饴(《事类赋》及《越旧经》所引皆作"味若饴"),令我采葛以作丝(《文选》注引采葛妇诗有'饥不遑食四体疲'一句,此书无之,缺文也),女工织兮不敢迟。弱于罗兮轻霏霏,号绨素兮将献之。越王悦兮忘罪除,吴王欢兮飞尺书。增封益地赐羽奇,机杖茵褥诸侯仪。群臣拜舞天颜舒,我王何忧能不移?"

以上引文中的"此书"指《吴越春秋》。此歌词首联及颔联起兴交代缘由,三联描述劳动情景,四连描写葛布质地,五联六联进献葛布产生的效果,末联表达必胜的信心。唯有如此,原文才合乎逻辑。

2. 关于歌的时代背景,本书认为歌的创作与流行当在勾践被释放回越之后、越国灭吴之前,而并非越妇在采葛之时所唱。理据是:其一,吴王"增封益地赐羽奇",是在"得葛布之献"之后;其二,歌中有"尝胆不苦甘如饴"一句,根据《史记》记载,卧薪尝胆的故事是发生在勾践返越之后;其三,"群臣拜舞天颜舒,我王何忧能不移?"二句,说明该歌产生时越国尚未灭吴,越王之忧尚未消除。

其六,"越王悦兮忘罪除"一句,若理解为"越王颇为欢喜,以至于忘记罪名已经免除",则甚不合乎文意与史实;窃思"除""馀"近形,或可通假。经查,果不其然。"除"可音除、音余或音舒。《康熙字典》之"除"字曰:"除馀字虽异,音实同也";《载敬堂集》云:"劳馀,犹工馀,劳作之馀。"古文"刑馀"指"受过刑的人",以此推而论之,则"罪馀"意即"戴罪之人"。据此,"越王悦兮忘罪馀"便是"越王如此高兴,以至于忘记自己是阶下之囚"之意了,英译如此处理似更为合理。

典籍英译确实是以审慎为妙。

其七,选译《吴越王还乡歌》,不免感慨系之。窃思人生价值多元,是否有善心善行,是否为民族和人类立功、立德、立言,为人处事是否刚正公允,以至于是否重视亲情友情,此乃其中之至要者也,岂可仅以权势与金钱衡人量物哉?

人来到世上,有的因祸国殃民、作恶多端而遗臭万年;有的因浑浑噩噩、醉生梦死而灰飞烟灭;有的则竭力尽智地追求和创造真、善、美,以使人类的家园更加温馨美好,即使不能流芳百世,却也生活得很有意义,令人景仰。概皆人生观、价值观使然也。

钱镠生活奢靡,然岂可苛责于古人、因其过而没其功耶?保境安民一事竟传颂千年,足见人心如镜。有今人秦舒《金华古子城侍王府感怀》一诗为证:

　　雄才不必凌烟阁,
　　大略何须五爪龙?
　　保境安民虽渺渺,
　　庭中双柏叶犹浓。

其八，关于瓦氏夫人的姓名，笔者曾发电子邮件请教百色学院的壮族学者陆勇先生。以下是他回复的大致内容：

关于"瓦氏夫人"姓氏问题，按照田阳县博物馆馆长黄明标的说法（他出有一书《瓦氏夫人研究》，广西民族出版社出版），瓦氏不是复姓，也不是她的姓，她实际上是田阳田州土官岑氏家族第十三世祖岑猛的妻子，夫家姓岑，按理叫岑夫人，姓岑，名花。但为何叫瓦氏夫人？原来，瓦氏是从靖西归顺州（今靖西县旧州镇）嫁到田州来的，她是该州土官岑璋之女，其小名为花。在当地，女孩取名后，经常要在其名前加上个衬词"氏"，男孩加衬词"于"，于是，瓦氏夫人就叫作"氏花"，她还有一个同胞姐姐叫"氏多"（史料有记载）。那她的名字怎么又变成了"瓦氏"呢？由于方言的不同，在旧州，"花"念"化"去声，而在田州方言"花"就念"瓦"三声，故她的名字来到田州就念为"瓦"，"氏花"就变成"氏瓦"了。

那为何"氏瓦"会变成"瓦氏"了呢？这个得从壮汉语法的倒置来解释。壮族习惯性先讲第一性，再说第二性，如汉语说"猪肉"，我们壮语要倒过来说"肉猪"。回到他们姐妹俩"氏多""氏瓦"，汉人一见便误以为这个"氏"是姓氏的"氏"，以为壮人受壮语表达习惯的影响，把"瓦氏"倒写成"氏瓦"，所以汉官就改"氏瓦"为"瓦氏"，这一误就误了几百年。

其九，龙山中学位于陆丰金龙山南麓，其前身为杭州籍陆丰县令陈张翼于1737年倡建、陆丰知县陈冠世于1742年（清乾隆七年）创建之龙山书院。关于龙山中学的优良传统和光辉历史，该校校友高阳懿的诗作或可资一管之窥：

木棉颂

龙山中学烈士纪念亭旁有百岁之木棉焉,苏世独立,高可数丈。每逢严霜肆虐,绿叶落尽,尤呈骨格清奇,且不攀不附,有君子固穷之高洁;及至惠风和畅,奇葩满树,更显心胸仁厚,况不傲不倨,无小人得志之轻狂。刚而正分,命蹇则修身砺志,蓄势待时,宁守七贤之节;慨以慷分,运转则含英咀华,赏心悦目,愿报三春之晖。咦,此诚吾辈忘年之益友、不语之良师也,岂只林中秀士、花间豪雄而已哉!龙山学子从其无言之教,因而崇德、笃学、明辨、力行以遂报国之志者亦众矣!适值六五届高中毕业五十周年,诸学友倡言以此嘉树为题,作画赋诗以志之,嘱余附合,乃成此草。

叶尽枝伤志未衰,兰心竹韵柏情怀。
千般苦雨清霜后,带露琼英向日开。

附录二:紫玉与韩重的生死恋——《搜神记》有关记载
Appendix II: The Romance of Ziyu — the Princess of Wu

吴王夫差小女,名曰紫玉,年十八,才貌俱美。童子韩重,年十九,在道术,女悦之,私交信问,许之为妻。重学于齐、鲁之间,临去,属其父母,使求婚。王怒,不与女。女结气死,葬阊门之外。

三年,重归,诘其父母。父母曰:"大王怒,女结气死,已葬矣。"重哭泣哀恸,具牲币往于墓前。玉魂从墓中出,见重,流涕谓曰:"昔尔行之后,令二亲从王相求,度必克从大愿，不图别后遭命，奈何。"玉乃左顾，宛颈而歌。歌毕，欷歔流涕，不能自胜，邀重还冢。重曰："死生异路，惧有尤愆，不敢从命。"玉曰："死生异路，吾亦知之。然今一别，永无后期，子将畏我为鬼而祸子乎？欲诚所奉，宁不相信？"重感其言，送之还冢。玉与之饮宴，留之三日三夜，尽夫妇之礼。临出，取径寸明珠以送重，曰："既毁其名，又绝其愿，复何言哉！愿郎自爱。若至吾家，致敬大王。"

重既出，遂诣王，自说其事。王大怒曰："吾女既死，而重造讹言，以玷秽亡灵。此不过发冢取物，托以鬼神。"趣收重。重走脱，至玉墓所，诉之。玉曰："无忧，今归白王。"

王妆梳，忽见玉，惊愕悲喜，问曰："尔缘何生？"玉跪而曰："昔诸生韩重来求玉，大王不许。玉名毁义绝，自致身亡。重从远还，闻玉已死，故赍牲币，诣冢吊唁。感其笃终，辄与相见，因以珠遗之。不为发冢，愿勿推治。"夫人闻之，出而抱之，玉如烟然。

附录三：刘三姐的事迹与生平
Appendix III: The Life and Deeds of Liu Sanjie

刘三姐，本名刘三妹，相传为唐代人，聪颖过人，出口成章，系民间传说中的歌仙。有关她的记载最早见于南宋王象之（1163—1230）《舆地纪胜》卷九十八之"三妹山"。明清以来，有关她的传说与歌谣的记述、评论很多，壮族民间口耳相传的故事与歌谣则更为丰富。

1. 明末清初著名学者屈大均在他的《广东新语》中有关于刘三姐（即刘三妹）的如下记载（本书加以标点，并将繁体字简化）：

新兴女子有刘三妹者，相传为始造歌之人，生唐中宗年间。年十二,淹通经史,善为歌。千里内闻歌名而来者,或一日,或二、三日,卒不能酬和而去。三妹解音律,游戏得道,尝往来两粤溪峒间。诸蛮种类最繁,所过之处咸解其言语,遇某种人即依某种声音,作歌与之唱和。某种人奉之为式。尝与白鹤乡一少年登山而歌,粤民及瑶、僮诸种人围而观之,男女数十百层,咸以为仙。七日夜歌声不绝,俱化为石。土人因祀之于阳春锦石岩。岩高三十丈许,林木丛蔚,老樟千章蔽其半。岩口有石磴,苔花绣蚀,若鸟迹书。一石状如曲几,可容卧一人,黑润有光,三妹之遗迹也。月夕辄闻笙鹤之音,岁丰熟则仿佛有人登岩顶而歌。三妹今称歌仙,凡作歌者,毋论齐民与狼、瑶、僮人、山子等类,歌成必先供一本,祝者藏之,求歌者就而录焉,不得携出。渐积遂至数箧,兵后今荡然矣。(中国基本古籍库,《广东新语》,第144页)

2. 清人吴淇等编撰的清康熙二年刻本《粤歌续九》有"歌仙刘三妹传"。兹将有关文字转化为简化字,将按语、注释置于括号之内并以小号字体呈现,并加以标点,转录于此:

歌仙名三妹,其先汉刘晨之苗裔。流寓贵州,即今浔州府贵县(非贵州布政)西山水南村。父尚义,生三女,长大妹,次二妹,皆善歌,早适有家而歌不传。少女三妹生于唐中宗神龙五年己酉。(按:唐中宗神龙三年即改元景龙,云神龙五年,误。宜作景龙三年。)甫七岁即好笔墨,聪明敏捷,时呼为女神童。年十二,通经史,善为歌。父老奇之,试之,顷刻立就。十五艳姿初成,歌名益盛,声以色重,千里之内闻风而来。或一日,或二日,率不能和而去。十六,其父纳邑人林氏聘,来和歌者仍终日填门,虽与酬答不拒,而守礼甚严也。十七,将于归,有邕州(即今南宁府)白鹤乡少年张伟望者,美丰容,读书解音律,造门来访。言谈举止皆合歌节,乡人敬之。（敬字描粤人重歌，性情如化）工筑台西山之侧，令两人登台为三日歌。台阶三重，干以紫檀，幕以彩段，百宝流苏，周乎四角。三妹服鲛室龙鳞之轻绡，色乱丽霞，头作两丫，鬓丝发散垂至腰，曳双缕之宝带，躡九凤之纹履，双眸盼然，掩映九华扇影之间。少年着乌纱，摇衣绣衣，执节而立于右。是日风清日丽，山明水绿，粤民及猺獞诸种人围而观之，男女数百层，咸望以为仙矣！两人对揖三让，少年乃歌《芝房》之曲，取灵芝无根之意，以美刘也。三妹答以《紫凤》之歌，紫凤属离方，取其文彩以报张也。观之人莫不叹绝。少年复歌《桐生南岳》，张还以凤比刘，以桐自比，待其来栖之意。三妹以《蝶飞秋草》和之，恨其相逢之晚，己已受聘，若蝶不及春花而秋草也。少年忽作变调四歌……

所有这些不仅有助于了解歌者及其作品，而且为本书的编排提供了凭据。

附录四：2015典籍翻译高层论坛欢迎词（节选）
Appendix IV: Speech at the 2015 Summit Forum on the Translation of Classics (excerpt)

"上善若水"，典籍翻译就是上善之举，功耀当代，德照千秋。在物欲横流的社会里，大家苏世独立，选择了典籍翻译与研究，这是学术界文化自信、文化自尊和社会责任意识的体现，也是中国译学的希望之所在。

我在2001年建立首家典籍英译研究机构，首倡建立全国典籍英译研究会，并于翌年和兄弟院校的学者一道将倡议付诸实施。此后，典籍英译与研究这个学科方向逐步形成，典籍翻译与研究这支文化新军茁壮成长。全国的同道同仁在学术上攻城略地，遇到、解决并正在解决前所未有的理论与实践问题，硕果累累，功勋卓著。与此同时，大批青年才俊得以茁壮成长。这是祖国之幸，也是世界之幸！

朋友们，典籍外译任重道远，我们正面临着新的问题和挑战：

1. 创新与精英密度有关（比如硅谷、中关村）。各省各兄弟院校能否汇聚人才，建立研究机构，加强校际学术联系与交流，把翻译、编撰地方文库的工作做起来？

2. 在学术共同体的管理机制方面，是君主制、禅让制好，还是民主制好？应相互尊重包容，形成学派，还是相互挤压排斥，形成宗派？

3. 在学理、学养、学风方面，是崇洋媚外，对蜂拥而至的"绣花枕头"（如季羡林先生所言）顶礼膜拜，鹦鹉学舌，抄袭克隆，从事学术造假、理论造假，还是树立民族学术自尊、学术自信，以中国文论为体，以西方译论为用，立志创新求变？是急功近利、粗制滥造、以量取胜，还是如切如磋、精益求精、严谨治学？在新时期典籍外译史的研究方面，是秉公持论，还是说谎造假、篡改历史？我们所要的是百家争鸣的"复调"局面，还是一家独揽天下的单调局面？

4. 在元典的复译方面，应建立、遵循什么道德伦理标准和法规？原译者的学术贡献和复译者的学术创新应如何评判？原译者在复译作品中应享有什么分量的知识产权？如何判断、防止复译中的抄袭？

诸如以上的问题，希望能引起学者们的关注。

……

秉壮士烈女之如虹正气，叨圣哲先贤之似日灵光，中华民族方得以生存发展，华夏文化方臻于如此博大精深。吾辈宁不思其流泽乎？宁不爱我尧天舜土以慰先贤先烈的在天之灵乎？宁不扬其光以奋发前行乎？

朋友们，让我们继续与亿万同胞一起，充分认识东方文明的价值，增强文化认同感，保持自己的文化身份，捍卫自己的文化安全和国家安全，以实现我华夏文化之复兴！

卓振英
2015年6月6日

主要参考文献
References

1. 北京爱如生数字化技术研究中心．中国基本古籍库［DB］．合肥：黄山书社，2007．
2. 陈昌义．外来词为载体的西方文化对汉民族文化的冲击［J］．浙江师范大学学报．2003（1），102-103．
3. 冯明洋．越歌：岭南本土歌乐文化论［M］．广州：广东人民出版社，2006．
4. 黄现璠、黄增庆、张一民．壮族通史［M］．南宁：广西民族出版社，1988．
5. 郭著章、江安、鲁文忠．唐诗精品百首英译［C］．武汉：武汉大学出版社，2010．
6. 李贻荫．谈《玉台新咏》英译本［J］．读书．1998（3），68-73．
7. 梁庭望、廖明君．布洛陀——百越僚人的始祖图腾［M］．北京：外文出版社，2005．
8. 马明蓉、戎林海．《越人歌》的审美再现——从语内翻译到语际翻译［J］．常州工学院学报．2016（3），57-61．
9. 裘士雄．越歌百曲［C］．香港：天马图书有限公司，2001．
10. 沈雨梧．太平天国浙江歌谣选［C］．金华：太平天国侍王府纪念馆，1982．
11. 万彩玲．情歌？同性恋歌？颂歌？——《越人歌》性质探析［J］．安徽文学．2008（6），114-115．

12. 汪榕培等. 吴歌精华［C］. 苏州：苏州大学出版社，2003.
13. 王宏印. 中国古今民歌选译［M］. 北京：商务印书馆，2014.
14. 余姚县委宣传部华东师大政治教育系. 四明山革命歌谣选［C］. 杭州：东海文艺出版社，1959.
15. 中国作家协会浙江分会筹委会. 浙江歌谣［C］. 北京：人民文学出版社，1960.
16. 朱秋枫. 浙江歌谣源流史［M］. 杭州：浙江古籍出版社，2004.
17. 朱秋枫. 浙江民间歌谣散辑［C］. 上海：上海文化出版社，1956.
18. 卓振英. 大中华文库·楚辞（英译）［C］. 长沙：湖南人民出版社，2006.
19. 卓振英. 汉诗英译论纲［M］. 杭州：浙江大学出版社，2011.
20. 卓振英. 美国幽默经典读本［M］. 上海：华东理工大学出版社，2011.